Accidental Proposal

By Kenadee Bryant

Accidental Proposal

Copyright © 2016 by Kenadee Bryant.
All rights reserved.
First Print Edition: September 2016

Limitless Publishing, LLC
Kailua, HI 96734
www.limitlesspublishing.com

Formatting: Limitless Publishing

ISBN-13: 978-1-68058-800-2
ISBN-10: 1-68058-800-1

Dedication

To the one person who knew me the best, Ruben. Even though you aren't here anymore, I know you would be happy for me. I love you.

Chapter One

Jenna

For most people, life doesn't turn out the way they planned. They don't end up with their high school sweethearts, or they don't go to their dream college. For me, nothing in my life has turned out the way I wanted it to. I didn't think I would be dropped off at an orphanage when I was just five years old, or that I would just barely graduate high school, or that I would be working two awful jobs just so I could pay rent. You could say my whole life so far has been one big disappointment.

"Jenna, you're needed at table three!" someone shouted, interrupting my thoughts. Sighing, I stood up from my stool and headed to my table. I hated my job. Well, actually, I "disliked" my job. The small diner where I worked, Ruby's, was a dive. The paint was chipped and peeling away. The booth seats had holes in them and crayon marks from little kids. There was always something wrong with the place, but people seemed to keep coming. I guess

1

the only really good thing about the diner was the food. It was pretty good, compared to the decor. I've been working here for almost a year, and nothing has changed.

After serving the older man at table three some coffee, I went and sat back down. It was a Monday morning, so it was super slow. I already wanted it to be the weekend, but the week had only just started. Hell, it wasn't even ten o'clock yet. I was looking forward to finally having a weekend off, since I'd worked the last three. I haven't been this thankful for Friday in a long time. All I wanted to do was sleep in until noon and lie around in my PJs.

I ran my hand through my dirty blonde ponytail as I looked around the diner. There were only three customers scattered around, drinking coffee and reading the newspaper. Most of them were older people who came here every other day. With a sigh, I lay my head on my hands. I hadn't gotten any sleep last night. I was ready to take a nap right here on the counter.

"Why so tired?" I heard Sophia, my only friend here at the diner, ask. "Long night?" She looked at me from behind the counter and started to wipe the surfaces with a wet towel.

"You could say that. I ended up having to stay until four at the club last night to close and clean up. Then I had to be here at six to open," I said, stifling a yawn. Sophia was the only person who really knew anything about me and my past. I was usually closed off from everyone, but Sophia had wormed her way into my life and stuck. She's a good three to four years older than I am, with short blonde hair and the prettiest blue eyes I have ever seen.

"Girlie, you work too hard. You need time to rest," she said, giving me a condescending look. At times, Sophia likes to act like my mother, even though she isn't that much older than I am.

"I'm fine, Soph. Plus, I need the money to pay bills."

"If you need money, ask Pete for a raise. He might give it to you." Pete is the owner of the diner. He's a huge guy, standing at six-foot three and about two hundred thirty pounds, if not more. His once-brown hair has started to turn grey, and he's got a few more wrinkles these days. Even at sixty-one, he looked younger. He still had muscle. I wouldn't want to find myself alone with him in an alley. But once I got to know him, I found out he is a big teddy bear. He'd do anything to help anyone.

"I can't do that. This place doesn't do well enough for me to get a raise. I'll just keep working more hours here and at the club. It's fine," I said, shaking my head. I couldn't borrow money. I wasn't that kind of person. I would rather be exhausted from earning money than borrow it from someone. I've been doing everything myself since I was fourteen, and that isn't about to change.

"Just think about it, okay?" she asked, looking at me pleadingly.

"I will, Soph. Thank you," I said, shooting her a small smile. Just then, the bell chimed above the door, announcing a new customer. Groaning in the back of my mind, I jumped off the stool and headed toward the front door.

Thankfully, the rest of the day went by pretty

fast. Before I knew it, my shift was over. Saying goodbye to Sophia over my shoulder, I left the diner and started walking to my apartment. I didn't live in the best neighborhood, but it's all I can afford. Thankfully, I didn't live too far from the diner. I only had to walk maybe a mile or so. It was mid-September, and it was starting to become chilly. I always dreaded the freezing cold of fall and winter in New York. The wind picked up a bit. I wrapped my thin jacket more tightly around me, as my uniform didn't cover much, leaving goose bumps up my legs and arms.

A few minutes later, my apartment came into view. I picked up my pace and soon entered my building. I climbed the stairs, reached my door, and slid my key in. Dropping my bag and jacket on my counter, I plopped down on my worn-out couch. I leaned my head back and let out a sigh as I sank into the cushion. Turning my head toward my clock hanging on the wall, I saw it was 2:30 p.m. I had about three hours before I had to change and head to the club. Along with my waitress job, I worked as a bartender at an exotic club down the road. Exotic was just a fancy word for a strip club. I honestly hated working there. I had to dress in short shorts and a tight tank top and had to wear makeup. Most of the customers I served would grab my ass or something. It wasn't a good job, but it paid well and I got tips added on top of that. Dressing in short, tight outfits and giving men flirty smiles might get me an extra hundred per night, if I was lucky.

I knew I wasn't old enough to sell alcohol, but the owner of the club lets me work. Teddy, the owner, is almost just like Pete from the diner. He's a big man with light brown hair with little grey specks in it. On the outside, he looks mean and scary, but he's nice to me and the other girls. He isn't one of those owners who doesn't care about his employees. He always asks us how we are and what we're up to. Teddy always seemed to have a soft spot for me. Instead of sending me away when I asked for a job, he made me promise I would only bartend, no drinking. If someone was messing with me, I could call one of the guards over immediately. I never have taken shit from anyone. Teddy's protective of all the girls, but slightly more so of me since I'm only nineteen.

I stared at the wall straight ahead of me, my thoughts drifting away. There was supposed to be a TV mounted where I was staring, but I didn't have enough money for one. I didn't even have a cell phone. Even during high school I didn't have a phone. The home didn't provide us with them. I didn't see the point in getting one when I only went from one job to another then back to my apartment. With no friends or family, I kept to myself and did what I had to.

The next couple of hours passed quickly. Before I knew it, I had to get in the shower and get ready. As I stood under the warm water, I closed my eyes and let the water cascade over me. I didn't get the chance to shower when I got home that morning, so the water felt great. I quickly washed my long blonde hair and my body, not wanting to be late. Reluctantly, I turned off the shower and stepped out, wrapping myself in a towel. I dried myself off and wrapped the towel around my head as I got dressed. When I first started at the club, I didn't have the "right" clothes, so Teddy had one of the girls take me shopping to get "sexy" clothes, as she called them.

I got dressed in my black shorts, which were almost like spandex, and a tight white tank top that showed an inch of my skin below my navel. Like a normal person, I slipped on my cheap black Converse instead of heels. I didn't wear heels. Heading back to the bathroom, I brushed my hair and pulled it into a high ponytail, even though it was still wet. When I looked in the mirror at myself, I sighed. My green eyes were the same dull color, but the bags under them made me look older than I was. Every time I looked at myself in the mirror, I couldn't help but feel disgusted with what I saw. I looked just like my mother. I had her eyes and face shape. Maybe if I didn't look so much like her, maybe she wouldn't have left me. Before I could depress myself, I grabbed my bag and jacket and left my apartment, making my way to the club.

I walked quickly to the club, the chilly wind biting at my bare legs. Five minutes later, I rounded the corner and caught sight of the big **'Tammy'** sign above the entrance of the club. I went to the side door meant for employees and tapped on it. It slid open to reveal Tom's face, staring down at me. All the guards at the doors and around the club were huge. Teddy hired the best "bodyguards" to protect us, in case some customers got too handsy.

"Hey, Tom," I said, smiling at him as he let me inside the warm room.

"Hi, Jenna. Nice to see you. How are you this evening?" he asked, shutting the door and looking over his shoulder at me.

"I'm good. How are you? How is Kendra?" I asked, slipping my jacket off and hooking it on the coat rack by the door. Kendra was Tom's long-time girlfriend. They'd been together for years, but he'd never married her and I didn't know why. I'd met her a few times, and she was super nice and cool to talk to.

"I'm doing good. Kendra is good as well. Just driving me nuts, as always," he said, smiling.

"You better put a ring on her before she gets some common sense and leaves you," I joked as I walked backwards toward the door leading to the bar. Tom has always been my favorite guard, and we both loved to give each other a hard time. The best part is, we can both take it.

"Yeah, yeah. Whatever. You better shut your trap before I leave you out in the cold next time." He gave me a look, but I just laughed.

"You wouldn't. You love me, Tommy," I said, sending him a wink and a wave as I left and headed to the bar to start my shift. I slipped behind the bar and saw Candy was working with me today. Most of the girls here were nicer than they appeared. Actually, most of the girls who worked here were just here to pay for school, or for their children, or even just for some cash. Candy was one of those who worked her to support her four-year-old daughter, Sky. She got pregnant when she was seventeen, and her high school boyfriend left her the moment he found out. Now, at twenty-one, she

7

had to raise her daughter on her own, and her kid is one of the cutest kids I've ever met by far. She's got the best manners for a four year old, and she always makes me laugh when I see her.

"Hey, Candy!" I practically shouted over the loud music.

"Hey, Jenna. You're working again?" she asked, pouring vodka into a glass, then some water. She worked with me yesterday but got off four hours before I did.

"Yeah, I am. But I'm off at eleven," I said, then got to work on someone's drink. Pouring whiskey into a glass, I slid it across the bar and grabbed the money the man laid down. One after another I poured drinks and collected the money. Before I worked here, I didn't know there were so many kinds of drinks. There were Sip and Go Naked, Buttery Nipples, Rum and Coke, Margaritas, all different kinds of beers, etc. I would be lying if I said I'd never drank before, but that was only once, when I graduated and got dragged to a party by one of the other kids in the home. I drank way too much and ended up with a terrible hangover. After that, I vowed to never drink again. Plus alcohol never tasted good to me.

For the next hour I made one drink after another, never having a break. Thankfully the girls would put on a show on the top of the hour, leaving us bartenders free for about thirty minutes or so. Since this was a strip club, every hour a handful of girls would go up on stage and "perform" for the gentlemen. I usually took that time to run to the bathroom and wash up. When it got super busy, the drinks usually splashed up on your arms, making your arms and hands sticky and smelling like whatever you were serving. As I wiped the counter down, I felt like someone was watching me. I looked out of the corner of my eye and saw Candy was doing the same thing. Frowning, I kept wiping the counter until all the alcohol spills were cleaned up. I took a step back and pulled down my tank top, which had ridden up. I ignored the feeling of being watched when a man walked up to the bar.

"What can I get you?" I asked, setting my rag down.

"You can give me a lap dance." He shot me a white-toothed smile. I watched as he looked down my body but stopped at my stomach. The counter blocked the rest of his view. The way he was looking at me made my skin crawl.

"Sorry, not my job. You can go ask one of the girls over there," I said, gesturing to the right of the bar where the girls who usually did lap dances stood. I turned away from him to another customer. The new guy wanted a beer, so I turned around and grabbed a glass to pour it in. As I poured his drink, the creepy guy stood there staring at me. Trying to act like I wasn't getting freaked out, I handed the new guy his beer with a smile.

"Jenna, there's a guy over there that wants you to bring him his drink," Candy said, sliding up next to me.

"What? Why?" I asked, confused. Usually the men just came to us.

"I don't know, but he specifically asked for you. So here," she said, handing me a whiskey and nodding toward the section the "guy" was sitting in. I was silently glad to get away from the creepy guy. I passed Candy and exited behind the bar on her side, heading to the customer with his drink. The lights were down, so it was kind of hard to tell who I was supposed to go to, but when I edged around a table, I saw a pair of bright blue eyes staring straight at me. My legs immediately felt glued to the floor. Even from here I could see his face, and to say he was gorgeous was an understatement. He had high, prominent cheekbones and a jaw-line sharp enough to cut someone. His blue eyes were bright and intense as he stared at me. I finally forced my legs to move, somehow knowing he was the person who ordered the drink.

"Here you go," I said quietly, setting the whiskey down. Being near him, I realized he was even more handsome. Instead of thanking me, he just nodded, his eyes hard. Slightly taken aback, I also nodded and turned away. I frowned as I walked back to the bar. *Why would he ask me to bring him his drink and not say anything? Wait, why do I even care?* Shaking off thoughts of the mysterious man, I got back behind the bar, thankful the creepy guy was gone.

The rest of the night went by quickly, with nothing else weird happening. The mysterious hot man either left or didn't order anymore drinks, and the creepy guy was gone, but that still didn't mean I didn't get hit on. Once the clock hit eleven, I stepped back and Stacey, the girl taking over for me, took my spot and started serving drinks.

"I'm off. I'll see you tomorrow," I called over to

Candy. She smiled and waved at me over her shoulder. I weaved past drunken men toward the side door for my jacket. When I pushed through the door, I saw Tom. "You're still here?" I asked, grabbing my jacket and putting it on. I could already feel myself shivering, and I hadn't even stepped outside yet.

"Yeah, I'm here until closing," he said, smiling over at me. "Do you want me to call you a cab?" he asked and went to open the door for me.

"No, that's okay. I'll walk, but thank you. I hope you have a good night, Tommy," I said. I shot him a smile at him and slid past him, hearing him shout "Goodbye and be careful" as I walked away from the club. As the cold air blew, I shivered in my thin jacket, picking up my pace. I did not want to be out here longer than I had to. Suddenly, a car pulled up beside me. Like an idiot, I stopped dead in my tracks. A minute later, the door opened and a tall figure stepped out. When a streetlight illuminated the figure's face, I tried not to gasp. It was the stranger from the bar.

Chapter Two

I stood there, in the middle of the sidewalk, as the stranger walked up to me. I had to tilt my head back so I could see his face. He must be six-foot two or six-foot three, much taller than my five-foot four height. He looked a few years older than me, maybe twenty-four or so. My voice seemed to be stuck in my throat. His blue eyes stared down at me, almost making me cower. Standing this close to him was intimidating, especially after seeing what he was wearing: a clean-cut black suit jacket, a white button-up shirt underneath, with a dark blue tie that made his blue eyes darker, and a pair of black slacks with shiny black dress shoes. His brown hair was styled perfectly, not a strand out of place, and he had a five o'clock shadow covering his chin and cheeks. His lips looked so kissable I nearly jumped on him. Everything about him screamed wealth and power. I could just feel the power radiating off of him as he practically glared at me.

"I need you to come with me," he said, his voice deep and velvety. Finally, after staring at him for a good couple of minutes, I spoke up.

"W-what?" I stuttered out, confused. *This mysterious, handsome man wants me to get in the car with him? Is he crazy?* I looked him up and down, trying to find any sign of him being crazy, but didn't find anything except a very expensive Rolex watch. Okay, not crazy, just crazy rich maybe.

"I need you to come with me," he said again slowly, as if talking to a little kid. Hearing him talk down to me seemed to jerk me awake.

"Excuse me? I am not going anywhere with you. I have no idea who you are. And don't talk down to me as if I'm stupid or a child," I said, narrowing my eyes at him. I crossed my arms over my chest as I glared up at him. I could see him clenching his jaw, his lips thinning as if he was trying not to yell.

"Jenna, I need you to come with me. I have something to discuss with you." His voice was hard. *How does he know my name?* He must have seen the look on my face, because he said, "I was at the club, remember?" *Ohhhh.*

I stood there in silence, having an internal war with myself. One part of me wanted to go and see what he wanted, while the other was shouting a warning at me, saying, "Don't go!" *Maybe he wants something from you?* a voice said in the back of my mind. The thought of sleeping with this handsome stranger somehow seemed to turn me on. *Jenna, get your shit together!* "Jenna, I promise you I will not harm you. All I want to do is talk to you for a few minutes. Then I'll bring you back home," the stranger said, interrupting my thoughts. The longer

13

we stood out in the cold wind, the weaker my resolve became.

"Are you a rapist?" I asked him.

"No."

"Are you a killer?"

"No."

"I will only get in the car if you tell me your name."

"Liam. Liam Stanford," he said, raising an eyebrow at me almost expectantly. *What? Did he think I would immediately trust him or know his name?* I thought angrily. He stepped to the side and gestured to the car. Sighing, I walked to the car, no longer able to feel my hands or toes. Liam opened the door for me as I slid inside. Liam slid in next to me and gestured with his hand. I then noticed that there was a driver in the front seat. *Wow, he does have a lot of money.*

I stared out the window as we drove down the street, headed to who-knew-where. The car was quiet. I should be scared driving with an unknown man headed to an unknown location, but for some reason, I really wasn't…Stupid, I know. After about ten minutes of complete silence, we pulled up to Liam's destination. The moment the car came to a stop, Liam opened the door and stepped out. Now slightly scared, I slowly slipped out and stood beside him. I quickly looked around and almost sighed in relief. We were out front of a coffee place. While I was busy looking around, Liam had already walked to the front door of the coffee shop and was impatiently waiting for me. I was already done with his attitude. I walked past him and instantly smelled the amazing aroma of fresh ground coffee. Not bothering to wonder why this place was still open at 11:30 at night, I walked to the front counter.

"Hi," I said to the bored-looking barista. She was about my age, maybe a year older. She had platinum-dyed hair and makeup caked on her face, making her look like an Oompa Loompa.

"Hi," she said boredly.

"I'll have a hot chocolate…grande," I said, not wanting coffee so late. I planned on listening to Liam for just a few minutes, then heading home to pass out before waking up at nine for my diner shift.

"Is that all?" the barista asked, punching something in on the computer.

"No. I'll have a coffee…grande." I heard Liam's deep voice come from behind me. The moment he spoke, the girl immediately perked up and plastered a smile on her make-up-caked face.

"Do you want anything else?" she asked, pushing her chest out, obviously hoping to get Liam's attention. I couldn't help but roll my eyes.

"No," came his curt reply. The girl didn't seem to get the hint but at least rang us up. I reached into my bag and pulled out some money. Before I could hand the money over, a big hand shoved mine away and handed the girl cash. I looked up at Liam, who was now pressed against my side.

"I was going to pay," I objected.

"I got it," was all he said before walking toward a table a few feet away. Since we were the only people in the shop, we didn't have to give the girl our names. I took a seat across from Liam, starting to wonder what he wants to talk to me about. *I don't even know him. I just found out his name not even fifteen minutes ago. What would he want to talk to me about?* We sat in silence as we waited for our drinks. A few minutes later, the barista came over with them. She practically threw mine at me while handing Liam his, her breasts practically in his face. When she walked away, I saw she had written her number on the side of his cup. It didn't surprise me, and it still wouldn't if Liam called her.

"So what did you want to talk to me about?" I finally asked, taking a sip of my hot chocolate.

"I want you to be my wife," Liam said bluntly. I choked on my hot chocolate and sat there coughing, my eyes wide.

"W-What did you just say?" I asked once I finally stopped coughing.

"I want you to be my wife," he said again, taking a sip from his coffee and staring at me like he had just asked me what my favorite color was, instead of asking for my hand in marriage. I started to laugh. *This is a joke. He's definitely kidding.* "Why are you laughing?" he asked almost angrily.

"Because you're joking." When he didn't agree with me, I stopped laughing. "Are you being serious? We don't even know each other! Hell, I just met you twenty minutes ago!" I yelled.

"Keep it down!" he hissed at me, his voice low and dangerous.

"How can you ask me that after you just practically proposed to me?" I hissed back at him. My hands tightened on my cup. "You have to be joking right now, Liam. I am not going to marry you!"

"Yes, you will. I am not asking you to be my wife forever. I am asking you to be my wife for a year. Nothing more, nothing less."

"Why do you want me? You can have any girl you want," I said.

"Because I need someone who will make my parents think I've changed. I need someone that is the opposite of my usual girls," Liam said, shrugging as he drank from his cup. *"Someone that is the opposite of my usual girls?" Yeah, that makes me feel so good. Glad to know I'm at the bottom of your pretty list.*

"Why do you need someone to make your parents think you've changed?" I asked, confused. *Why would his parents care?*

"You don't know who I am, do you?" he asked, switching the subject suddenly.

"No…am I supposed to?"

"Does Stanford Industries ring a bell?" I vaguely remembered hearing that name before, but I didn't know what it was or what it had to do with Liam. The look I gave him said no.

"I own Stanford Industries, well, my family does. My name is very well known in New York." He went on when he saw I still didn't know what he was talking about. "My company owns multiple hotels, apartment buildings…ring any bells?"

"Not really," I answered truthfully. What? I didn't get out much. He sighed and rubbed his forehead.

"Anyways, I want you to be my wife so I can show my father I am the right choice to take over the company."

"You want me to marry you so you can take over your father's company. And to be only married for a year. Am I right?" I asked, trying to figure out why he wanted me to marry him.

"Yes. You won't be left without anything after the year. When the year has passed, we will get a divorce and you will get a million dollars." I almost choked again. He mentioned it as if it were only ten dollars.

"Are you kidding me? A million dollars?" A million dollars was a lot of money. *How can he just hand that kind of money over to someone?*

"Money is not an issue for me," was all he said.

How rich are you? I wanted to say but bit my tongue. *How stupid could I be to say yes? But a million dollars! You could do things you've always wanted to do, and you could quit your awful jobs.* I sat there, arguing internally with myself. Liam sat silently, seemingly letting me think about his offer as he sipped his coffee.

"Can I think about it and let you know?" I finally asked. I wanted to say no, but some part of me wanted me to think about it. Money like that was something I didn't want to immediately say no to, especially in my situation. I would never be able to save up that much.

"Yes, you may. Here is my number. Let me know when you have decided," Liam said, handing me a business card. He stood up and waited for me to get up and follow him. Holding onto the card, I grabbed my cup and followed Liam outside to the car. He slid in beside me and looked over at me. "Your address."

"184 Burton Street," I said, feeling ashamed about my neighborhood. He repeated the address to the driver, and the car started back to my apartment. Thankfully, Liam didn't say anything about me living in a pretty bad neighborhood or that I lived close to the club. A few minutes later, we pulled up to the front of my building.

"Thank you for the drink and ride back," I said, opening the car door.

"You're welcome. Think about my proposal. I want a reply by the end of the week at the most," Liam said, turning to me. I frowned at his formal answer and the way he was talking to me. I held back an eye roll and got out of the car. Closing the door, I made my way inside my apartment.

During the entire walk to my place, I kept replaying what Liam told me. How could I marry some stranger I just met, and for money? When I got inside my apartment, I threw away my drink and changed out of my clothes. I crawled into my comfortable bed and stared up at the ceiling. Even though I have been up since six this morning and didn't go to bed until four, I was now wide awake. When I looked at my clock, I saw it was midnight. I knew I should try and go to sleep because I had to be at work at nine, but everything that had happened tonight ran through my mind. The crazy part about it all was I was really considering taking Liam's deal.

***

The next day at work, I was almost in a daze. I

hadn't been able to sleep all night, and I couldn't stop thinking about Liam's proposal. The idea of marrying someone I didn't even know wasn't appealing, but that kind of money was. People would probably think I'm a gold digger, but since I've been on my own most of my life, I have never had anything nice or anything that wasn't a necessity. I could maybe have a life.

All the pros and cons ran through my head as I went from table to table. I was starting to think I was crazy for even considering the deal. What would even happen to me during this year? Would Liam expect me to act like I'm some high-class lady? To act like I was madly in love with him? And what if someone found out this was all a hoax? Plus, what would happen to me at the end of the year marriage? All these questions came to mind throughout the day. *But it's only for a year.* My shift ended at 5 p.m., and I sat on a stool, thinking. Sophia kept asking what was on my mind, and I wanted to tell her, but I couldn't. I didn't want her to make me change my mind or to think I was crazy for considering this deal. After sitting there for five more minutes, I made my decision. I asked Sophia for her phone, and she gladly let me see it. Going into the back room, I dialed Liam's number.

"Hello?" he answered after three rings.

"Liam? This is Jenna Howard," I said nervously. I was about to make either the worst decision of my life or the best. "I will marry you."

Chapter Three

I didn't know that when I agreed to marry Liam, I would also be signing over my soul to the devil. A few days after I made the deal with him, a couple of big men came to my apartment around nine in the morning and started packing my things up. When I protested, they simply told me Mr. Stanford had paid them to come here and start gathering my stuff. They also mentioned that Liam wanted things to be mostly packed away by the end of the week. With it being Wednesday, that was practically impossible. Plus I didn't want some random guys going through my stuff. After a few minutes of arguing with the movers, well of me mostly threatening them, they agreed to come back tomorrow. The moment they left, I grabbed some quarters and left my apartment. I headed to a payphone down the street, fully intending on giving Liam a piece of my mind. *Man, I really need to get a phone,* I thought to myself as I put in some quarters and dialed the gross buttons. The moment Liam answered, I started yelling.

"Liam Stanford, what were you thinking? You

think you can send some random movers to my apartment and let them tell me I'm suddenly moving?"

"Jenna—" Liam started, but I cut him off.

"No, Liam, just because I agreed to be your fake wife does not mean you get to run my life! If you want me to move, you have to tell me directly. Now, why do you want me to move?" I ranted, pausing for a moment to hear his answer.

"You will be moving into my place with me." His answer was curt and rude. "I will resend the movers there to give you boxes to pack, and by Friday morning they will be moving all your stuff into my place. I do not want your furniture, so bring only your clothes. Leave everything else in boxes. You will need to quit your job at the club. 'My wife' would never be seen working there." There was a moment of silence, and I opened my mouth to protest, but he cut me off. "Oh, and Jenna…do not ever yell at me again." His voice was hard. With that, he hung up on me. I pulled the phone away from my ear and stared down at it.

What the—

***

The movers were back at my apartment an hour later with boxes to pack my stuff in. After telling them I did not need any help, I sent them away. I sat on my couch and just stared at the wall. Moving, quitting my jobs—so far agreeing to marry Liam was not turning out the way I wanted. Since I didn't have to work until two, I had a few hours before going to the diner. I started packing some of my things, beginning with the stuff in my bedroom, as I had the most stuff in there. I honestly didn't have much, and not moving my bed or couch into Liam's lessened the load.

About an hour and a half later, I sat on the floor with a few boxes all around me. My room looked practically bare, and I couldn't help but sigh.

"How pathetic. I already packed almost all my bedroom stuff and my bathroom, and it only took five boxes to do so," I said to myself. I left out the stuff I would need for the next two days, but the rest was already packed away. I guess when you didn't have money or a real home, you didn't need much to get by. *I may have to call Liam and have him bring the workers tomorrow instead of Friday.* Seeing the time, I got up and changed into my work uniform.

I wasn't looking forward to saying goodbye to the few friends I'd made at both my jobs. I'd miss them more than the job itself. I didn't even know what I was going to do when I was living with Liam, but I guessed I'd just have to find something to keep me occupied. I walked to Ruby's, trying to think of the best way of telling Pete I was leaving. *After my shift, I will.* I nodded. That sounded like the best option. Walking through the front doors, I breathed in the smell of the diner one last time. The scents of grease and hamburgers filled my nose. I smiled and made my way to the counter to put my stuff away. Thankfully Sophia was working today, so I could tell her goodbye. I didn't work tomorrow, and who knew when I would see her again, or if I'd see her at all after I left?

When I walked through the door, I saw almost all the tables were packed, with Sophia and the other two waitresses running around. Since it was practically lunch time, I quickly put my things away and grabbed my apron, tying it around my waist as I started helping at random tables. Seeing the diner packed like this was good, but I couldn't help but wonder what would happen when I left. Would there be enough workers? Would Sophia have to work even more? Instead of dwelling on those thoughts, I pushed them aside and helped out the customers.

For the next hour or so, I was busy going from one table to another, then back to the kitchen. I knew it was weird, but I was going to miss working here. The customers were usually very nice and knew who I was. Even after the rush died down and it was only me, Sophia, and this new girl, Vanessa, sitting around, I kept putting off telling Sophia and Pete all afternoon.

"Jenna, are you okay? You're quiet today," Sophia said, standing in front me.

"It's nothing," I said, playing with my fingers.

"Jenna." She had her hands planted on her hips as she stared at me. Sighing, I braced myself for her reaction.

"I am…quitting today," I said, peeking up under my eyelashes at Sophia.

"Wait? What? Why?" she asked, her voice high.

"I…it's a very long story."

"Well, you're in luck since we won't be busy for a while. Spill. Now." Her voice was hard. I nodded,

24

knowing I had to tell her. After I told her the whole story, I waited in silence as she mulled over everything I said. "Wow...just wow." I nodded in response. "So you're telling me *the* Liam Stanford asked you to marry him, only for a year, and for a million dollars?"

"Yes. Wait, do you know Liam?" I asked, picking up on the way she said his name.

"Duh! Everyone knows who he is. He is New York's most eligible bachelor and heartbreaker. He's known for being a cruel businessman and an award-winning heartbreaker. He's been with practically every model here and overseas. Come to think of it, I've never heard him being with someone longer than a week," Sophia said.

"Soph, that's not really helping," I said, feeling a pit in the bottom of my stomach. Just by his looks I knew Liam had been with many women, but the way Sophia was talking about him I now knew he'd been with more girls than what was in the tri-state area.

"Sorry, but how do you not know who he is? He's been on thousands of magazines, been on TV, even billboards." I just shrugged at her. All my money went to paying my bills, not for magazines or a television. "Anyways, Jenna, you are nuts! How could you agree to marrying him when you don't even know him?" she all but shrieked at me.

"I know, I know, but Soph, I need the money. I wasn't thinking clearly."

"Clearly you weren't," she interjected.

"But, it's too late to back out. And besides, who's going to get hurt? I do not plan on falling for this guy. I know he's attractive," I explained, putting my hand up to stop whatever she was going to say and continued, "but from what I've seen and heard from you, he isn't my type. I don't do men who break women's hearts for fun. Plus, I do not plan on falling in love ever, so I think I'll be fine."

"Jenna, I mean this in the nicest way possible...you are stupid. You are not going to make it out of this deal unscathed. You are going to end up hurt, and you've already been hurt enough." I tried to protest, but she stopped me. "I am not saying I am not going to be there for you the whole way, because I will. I'm just saying that you need to brace yourself for what may happen. Life isn't a fairytale. Not every princess ends up with a prince. I think this is a terrible idea, but I can see you are determined about this, so I won't try to convince you otherwise. If you ever need anything, just know I will always be here, okay?" she said, coming around the counter and pulling me into a big hug. I hugged her in return, thankful she had my back. I knew everything she said was probably true, but for now, I decided to ignore it.

After my shift, I went and told Pete I was quitting. When I apologized for the sudden notice, he simply pulled me in for a hug and told me if I ever wanted to come back, there would always be a spot for me. Trying not to tear up, I hugged him back and thanked him for everything. He told me to come by in a week for my paycheck and to also check in every once in a while. After one last goodbye to him and the other waitresses, I left. Sophia made me promise to get a cell phone right away and to give her my number when I came for my paycheck. We also made plans to meet up the following week.

As I walked home, I tried not to think about how much my life was changing. Once I got there, which was around eight that night, I decided to pack some more, since I had already eaten at the diner. I didn't have to work at the club tonight, so I planned on going in tomorrow after my shift and telling Teddy and Candy. It was pretty sad, how fast it took me to finish packing everything I owned. I didn't have any packing tape to tape the boxes, so if I needed anything in the next two days I could easily get it. After I had finished packing the last box, I looked around the apartment. Ten or eleven boxes total. The place seemed empty, even though the furniture was still here.

Since I was done packing, I was in for the night. I headed to the bathroom, undressed, and started the shower, waiting for it to get warm. I stared at myself in the mirror and almost squirmed. I wasn't the prettiest person out there. My blonde hair hung limply down in my face, and my green eyes were dull and almost lifeless, with big bags under them. My body wasn't spectacular either. I had round hips, and my thighs touched each other. My stomach was flat but only because sometimes I forgot to eat or couldn't afford to. I had a small scar on the top of my eyebrow from when I ran into a pole at school. All in all, I wasn't that easy on the eyes.

Jumping into the shower, I washed my hair and body and got out. I didn't want to waste too much water. After drying myself off, I got dressed in my comfy PJs and let my hair air dry. I crawled into my bed, grabbing my current book in the process. I spent the rest of the night reading and trying not to over think what I was doing with Liam.

***

I woke up the next morning around eight. About an hour later, the moving guys were back. Seeing as I was basically already packed, I asked one of the men if I could borrow their cell phone. *Note to self: Get cell phone as soon as possible.* I didn't realize how much I needed a phone until recently. Thankfully, the guy let me use his phone, and I dialed Liam's number. After a couple of rings, he picked up.

"Hello," his deep voice answered. Just the sound sent shivers down my spine.

"Hi, Liam. It's Jenna," I replied.

"Oh yes. Is there something you need?"

"Yes, I was wondering if you wanted me to move in today? I have all my stuff packed up already, and the movers are here."

"That would be fine. The movers know where to go. I will try to be there when you get there. What's the number I can call to let you know if I won't be there?" he asked.

"I, uh, I don't have a cell phone," I said, embarrassed.

"Okay, fine. I have to go, see you soon," was all he said as he hung up. Shaking my head, I turned and handed it back to the mover.

"Liam said you guys can move me into his apartment today," I told them. They nodded and asked where the boxes were.

"My bedroom. I don't have any tape, though."

"That's fine. We have some," the mover, whose phone I borrowed, said. They were quiet and quick as they followed me into my room and started taping up my boxes. They seemed pretty confused and surprised that I had so little. I remembered I still had to talk to the landlord, which I had completely forgotten about. I told the movers I would be right back.

My landlord was a slightly overweight lady in her late sixties. She always seemed pretty nice. I hoped it wouldn't be too complicated, getting out of my lease early. Feeling nervous as I walked downstairs and to her door, I hesitantly knocked. She answered a minute later.

"Hello?"

"Hi, Mrs. Whitman. I'm Jenna Howard from apartment 5B," I said.

"Oh hi, hon. What can I do you for?" she asked, opening the door and gesturing for me to enter. Smiling politely at her, I walked into her apartment and followed her to her couch.

"I know this a lot to ask, but I was wondering if I could get out of my lease early?" I still had about three months left, so I was hoping she would let me.

"Oh why's that, dear?"

"I...I have a sudden family emergency, and I am moving back home today," I lied. "I know it's so sudden. And you don't have to worry about the money for the lease or the rest of this month's rent.

The apartment is just how it was when I moved in and has furniture all in it."

"Oh, I am so sorry to hear that, honey. I hope everything is okay. But yes, that's all right. I know how important family is. I can give you back your deposit for the apartment. That isn't a big deal," she said kindly. I almost breathed out a sigh of relief, thankful she was going to let me get out of my lease. "I can give you that money in a week or so."

"Thank you so much, Mrs. Whitman. I will come and get that soon then," I said, giving her a thankful smile. I stood up, not wanting to keep the movers waiting.

"No problem, hon. I hope everything goes okay for you. When you leave, just put your key in my mailbox and I'll get it," Mrs. Whitman said kindly as she followed me to my door.

"Thank you. And you too." Saying goodbye, I went back to my apartment to grab the rest of my things.

I picked up the bag I'd put a few of my things in. Dressed in a pair of ripped jeans and a light blue t-shirt, I slung my bag over my shoulder and took one last glance around my apartment. Saying a silent goodbye, I walked out the door and shut it behind me, locking it. When I passed Mrs. Whitman's apartment, I set my keys inside her mailbox and went to meet the movers downstairs, who were standing there, waiting for me. It was slightly awkward as I slid inside the moving truck, being squished against the car door and the two big men.

About twenty minutes later, we pulled up next to a huge house, which was more like a mansion. I figured Liam would live in a big apartment in downtown, but instead he lived almost on the outskirts of the city. The house was almost square, with a white exterior. It looked and screamed bachelor pad. It had a five-car garage, and I bet it had a huge pool in the back too. I stood there, gawking at how nice the house was. When one of the movers walked in front of me, I forced myself to stop gawking. I followed the movers to the front door, which was open. I hesitantly stepped into the foyer and looked around. Everything was so neat and clean, and I felt so tiny and dirty just being inside. I blindly followed the movers, still glancing around at the place. The movers were just putting the boxes in the huge living room when I came to a stop in the middle of it.

Within just a few minutes, they were done and gone. I stood alone in the living room, surrounded by boxes. *Where's Liam?* I slowly walked around. A giant flat screen TV was hooked above on the wall, and below it was an impressive sound system. A leather couch sat on one side of the room, and a lounge chair was on the other side, a coffee table sitting in the middle. Just by looking at them, I knew they weren't cheap items. They probably cost over a grand each. Just as I was walking over to what looked like a good DVD collection, a voice stopped me in my tracks.

"Jenna," Liam said. I turned around, looking at him sheepishly. I knew I'd been caught practically snooping.

"Hi," I said awkwardly.

"I've brought documents that I need you to

31

sign."

"Documents?" I asked as I walked over to him.

"Yes. I need you to sign them immediately so I can make it official and get copies." He talked so business-like that, for some reason, it was starting to get under my skin. I'm his "fiancé". Shouldn't he talk to me normally, instead of like he's doing some business deal? He handed me the documents, which were encased in a folder. I turned to the couch to sit and read through them, although that didn't seem like what Liam wanted.

"All it says is that you will tell no one of our deal. And, after the one year, you will sign the divorce papers without any problems, and take what I promised you. After the year, I won't see you again or hear from you." I looked at him, almost apprehensively trying to decide if I trusted him enough not to read through it myself. Seeing as I really didn't have a choice and that I had no clue what I was doing, I took the pen Liam handed me and signed where I was supposed to.

"Good, now that is taken care of. First thing's first; when we are around my family or at any social events, I expect you to behave like any high-class person would. And you need to appear as if you are in love with me. Second, if you wish to have any male suitors, it needs to be done privately and secretly; I don't want people thinking my 'fiancé' is cheating on me. Third, this is not a real marriage. Do not expect me to be a loving and supportive husband, because I will not be either. When we are out in public, we will act like we love each other, but when we are by ourselves I do not want

32

anything to do with you. Also, don't plan on me sleeping with you because I will not. You will be sleeping in your own room, but everything in here is available to you. Remember this house is mine, so if I want to bring a woman back here, I want you to stay in your room or leave so they don't ask any questions. I get home late mostly every night or sometimes don't come home at all. Do not wait up for me or call me wondering where I am because I won't answer. You are to only call me if it is an emergency. We will tell my parents in a week's time, so be prepared," Liam explained.

"Also, I will hire someone to be your assistant who will dress you for important events and to get you a new wardrobe. No 'wife' of mine will wear clothes like what you've been wearing out in public. So far the press doesn't know about you, and I would like to keep it that way for a while, so don't go out in public for too long. I've deposited a hundred grand into your new bank account. You are welcome to use it. If you need more, just ask me. Here are your credit and debit cards." He handed me two black cards. "You told me you do not have a cell phone, so here you are. There is my number, my assistant's number, your driver's number, and when I get someone to be your assistant, I will give you her number to put in there. Now that is all. I am heading back to work, so unpack your boxes." After he was done, he just nodded at me and walked out the front door. I stood there in shock as I digested everything he'd said to me. I looked down and saw the brand new slick iPhone 6 in my hand, then looked back at the front door.

What the hell did I just do?

Chapter Four

I walked around Liam's place, awed. Never had I ever been in a place so big and nice. There were even two floors! There had to be four or five rooms, not including the master bedroom, with as many bathrooms, a huge laundry room, a gym, an office, a huge-ass kitchen, and, my favorite room, a library. The walls were stocked with every book you could think of and maybe even more; I knew I would be spending a lot of time in there.

As I predicted, out back there was a huge pool with a hot tub. The backyard was amazing with a weaving path almost like a maze that had all different kinds of flowers and plants. A little ways back toward the fence was a bungalow type thing, with a comfy bench and table. It was the perfect spot to come out to read, or just to think, really. Even though the house screamed bachelor pad, it had a bit of a feminine touch to it. The house seemed empty, like Liam wasn't here often. *Why have a nice house if you're not going to live there?*

I headed back inside to get started on unpacking

and finding a room I wanted. God knew there plenty to choose from. After looking at two rooms that were kind of small and didn't scream "me," I walked into the third bedroom down the hallway. The moment I walked through the double set of doors, I knew I wanted this room. A queen-sized bed sat in the middle with deep blue covers. On one side of it was a side table with a pretty lamp. Across from the bed to the right was an archway that led to a big walk-in closet that had built-in shelves for clothes or shoes, and straight across from the bed was another archway leading to a huge bathroom with a bath tub and walk-in shower. The counter was made of dark marble, and dark brown cabinets were beneath.

The room was easily twice the size of my old little apartment. I was glad I had doors leading to the outside; I could easily avoid Liam if needed. I stood in the middle of the room taking it all in, and a small smile appeared on my face. I may have signed my soul to the devil, but at least I would be living in a nice-ass place and getting money out of it.

The alarm on the bedside table showed it was almost eleven, so I decided I'd better get unpacking. It wouldn't take me long anyways. Going back down the hall, I found the living room, where I had left my boxes. I knew it was going to take a little while getting used to being in such a big place and not getting lost, with there being two separate hallways, one leading to the lower floor rooms, and the other to the laundry room and kitchen. There was a spiral staircase that led upstairs to Liam's room and the library. With a sigh, I picked up one box and headed back to my new room.

About an hour later, I stood there, glancing around the room with my hands on my hips. All my clothes were put away, which didn't even take up half the closet. What little belongings I had were placed throughout the room with the only picture I had of my mom and I, which we took two weeks before she left me. I had put my bathroom stuff away in the drawers and my toothbrush in a cool holder thing in the bathroom. The room still looked bare, but at least it looked slightly better than before. *With the money Liam put in my account, maybe I should get some more things for this room.* I was going to be here for a year, so I might as well make it as homey as I could. Plus, I had a feeling I would be in here quite a bit.

The growling of my stomach made me head back to the kitchen to find something to eat. When I entered the kitchen, I was once against impressed with the size and look of it—a flattop stove, double ovens, and a nice expensive stainless steel fridge. I bet the dark brown cabinets held nice cooking pots and pans, which were probably not even used. Hooked to the kitchen was a big room with a long dining room table that could seat about six people, maybe more. Instead of normal kitchen lights, Liam had dangling deep red glass lights. That was cool.

Opening the fridge, I glanced at its contents, trying to find something to eat. A lot of the food was in plastic containers and looked to be portioned out. I grabbed what looked to be spaghetti, shut the fridge, and started searching for a bowl. After opening five different cabinets, I finally found the one that held two different types of bowls as well as plates. Grabbing the first bowl I saw, I went to the drawer where I'd seen silverware earlier. I put the cold spaghetti in the bowl, and sliding it in the microwave, I washed the container as best I could before setting it in the dishwasher, knowing I couldn't get it all the way clean myself. When the microwave dinged, I took out the hot bowl and sat at the bar.

As I ate my spaghetti, I looked out the windows toward the backyard, thinking about my life. I never thought I would have to stoop as low as marrying a random guy for money. If my mother were here, I wondered if she would be ashamed of me. Just thinking of her made me sad and angry. Being only five years old and left alone in a new place, I'd felt like it was my fault my mom left me. Was I bad? Did I do something wrong? Of course, as I grew I went through different stages, from crying that it was my fault to hating my mother. I used to tell myself that she left for a good reason, that she wouldn't have abandoned me if she didn't have a choice. I even convinced myself for a few years that she was dead and that's why she didn't come back for me like she said she would. I mean, who would just leave their child at a doorstep and not want to come back for them?

Now, at the age of nineteen, I didn't care whether my mother was dead or alive. After years of wondering and blaming myself, I decided it didn't matter and that she was no longer my mother. She stopped being one the moment she left me at an orphanage. I'd once wanted to find my father, but with nothing to go on and my hidden hatred of him leaving my mother and me, I didn't do it.

There were plenty of times I wish I still had my mom. Like when a group of kids at the home would pick on me and I wanted to run to her to feel her arms around me, listening to her telling me things would be okay. Or when I went through my teenage years having to experience everything by myself and being confused when I got my first crush and the same boy being rude to me. Then at graduation, unlike most kids whose families had come and had people yelling for them when they went to receive their diplomas, I had no one there. I walked on the stage while a few people clapped, feeling bad for me. Then, when it was over and my friends went to their families, I handed in my gown and walked home alone. The couple that ran the orphanage couldn't come because they had to watch the little kids.

That night, after crying myself to sleep, I finally realized that I would always be alone. Over the years, I'd slowly come to accept that. What I said to Sophia about not ever falling in love was true. I had only ever had one boyfriend, and that was in my junior year of high school. We dated for almost a year before one day he told me at school he didn't want to see me again. Of course I was hurt beyond repair. It made me realize that everyone I love just left. The best way to not get your heart broken was to pretend like you didn't have one.

I hadn't been with anyone else since then, and I didn't plan on it either. This was the first time I had even gotten this close to a guy besides the ones from the club or the diner. Sure, Liam was attractive, very attractive, but with his cold demeanor and this deal, there wouldn't be anything happening between us.

My food was long gone, and it was nearing one. Since I didn't have to be at the club until five, I grabbed my new phone and headed outside to the backyard. Might as well play around with it to keep me busy before I had to get ready. Plus, it was nice outside for the first time in a while. We probably had only a few weeks before it started to become colder, and then it would be winter. Whenever it's warm in New York, you made sure to take advantage of the warm weather since it stayed cold for months.

I was kind of hot in my ripped jeans and light blue shirt as I sat down at the gazebo, looking down at my phone. Don't get me wrong, I knew I hadn't had a cell phone before, but I wasn't an idiot. I'd played around with my friend's phones, Sophia's and even Candy's. My friends in high school, Millie and Emily, always used to beg me to get a phone so I could get Facebook, that way we wouldn't stop being friends when they went off to college. All those girls in high school who made promises with their friends to stay friends forever should know it never happens. The moment they or you go off to college, everything changes. That person becomes someone different, and soon the texts between you become slower and smaller, until you don't talk to that person anymore.

Millie, Emily, and I were pretty close, but I

wouldn't say I was best friends with them. They had totally different lives than I did and didn't get why I was the way I am. After graduation, I only heard from them a few times, and after a few weeks we stopped talking altogether. They were planning on going to the same college together and getting an apartment. Of course those plans didn't involve me. I would like to say I felt hurt that I wasn't involved, but I really wasn't. What they wanted was not what I wanted.

I spent the next hour or so playing around on my phone, actually downloading Facebook and Instagram. I didn't really have anyone to add on either of them, but I might as well have them so I could stay busy. Setting my phone down on the bench beside me, I pulled my legs up to my chest and wrapped my arms around them. I laid my head on my knees and looked toward the house and the pool. The place was silent, besides the humming of a few bees and the slight breeze blowing through the trees. I closed my eyes and took a deep breath of the warm air.

Just being outside helped relax me, and I felt my head clearing. All I had to do was make it through this year, then I would be gone and out of Liam's life. *I can do this.* I stared out at the lawn, not really seeing anything. I kept trying to figure out how I was going to talk to Teddy and Candy. I hadn't really noticed it until now, but both of my jobs were so similar. At the diner I only had Sophia as my friend, and at the club I had Candy. Both of my bosses were practically the same as well. *Nothing gets by me,* I thought sarcastically to myself.

Noticing the time was nearing four already, I reluctantly stood up and headed back inside. I was not looking forward to tonight, and it didn't help that I didn't get off until one or so. As I was getting dressed in my short shorts and light blue tank top, I remembered Liam said I had a driver. Might as well call the number instead of having to take a taxi and pay for it. Once I was dressed and pulled my blonde hair up into a ponytail, I grabbed my phone and dialed the number that said "Driver". A second later, a young man's voice said hello through the phone.

"Uh, hi, I'm Jenna. Liam said you're my driver?" I said, or more like asked.

"Yes I am, miss. I'm Garrett. Is there something I can get you?" he asked.

"Um, yeah, I need to go to work. It wouldn't be a big deal for you to drive me there, would it?"

"No, ma'am, it wouldn't. I will be there in just a minute." Telling him thanks, I hung up and slid on my shoes before leaving my room and heading to the front door. I opened the front door just as a slick black car pulled up. Out stepped a tall, dark brown-haired guy who couldn't be more than three years older than I was. He walked around the car, toward me. I shut the door behind me and met him halfway.

"Hello, miss. I am Garrett." He extended his hand. Up close, I saw that he was very cute. He had dark brown hair that was kind of shaggy, his eyes were light brown, almost hazel, and he had high cheek bones with a sharp jaw. He smiled down at me, showcasing a set of white teeth.

"Hi, I'm Jenna." I shook his hand, smiling back

at him. He looked to be in his early twenties. I could feel his eyes roaming over my body before he looked me in the face.

"It's nice to meet you. So work, you said?"

"Yeah I have work at five."

"Well, let's get you there."

"Wait. I don't have any keys to lock the house up," I said.

"Don't worry. There's a keypad on the side by the door that locks the door after five minutes." I turned and saw what he was talking about. *Shit, this guy must have a lot of money to have an automatic keypad lock.*

"Oh, okay," I said. He walked to the car and opened the back door.

"Actually, would it be okay if I sat up front?" I asked. He looked surprised but nodded, opening the front door for me. I slid inside with a "thanks" before buckling up. Garrett came around to the driver's side, starting the car and heading down the driveway.

"Where to, miss?"

"You can call me Jenna. 224 South Morton Street." I hated when people called me miss, especially if Garrett was going be my driver for the next year. From the corner of my eye, I saw him raise an eyebrow, but he continued on anyways.

"Is Mr. Stanford your uncle? Or family friend?" he asked.

"Um…" I had no idea what to tell him now. I looked over at him, trying to see if I trusted him. "You can't tell anyone, okay?" If I'm going to be here for a while, I might as well try to have a friend.

"I won't. I promise."

"Okay…I'm his fake 'fiancé'."

"Fake?"

"Yeah. He offered me a deal, and I know it's crazy, but I took it," I said, leaning back in the seat, staring out the window.

"It may be crazy but…okay, I have nothing." I snorted at his response.

"That was an excellent answer."

"I think I know what he offered you, since you're dressed the way you are," Garrett said, looking over at me briefly then back at the road. We were getting closer to the club.

"Hey! I am not what you think I am. I'm a bartender at the club." He was quiet for a few minutes.

"Oh, that explains why you are so different than the other rich girls I've had to drive around."

"Other rich girls?"

"Yeah. I thought you were some daddy's girl who got everything she wanted. I was wrong." He shrugged.

"Well, thanks I guess," I said, getting where he was coming from. To anyone else, I probably looked like I was a spoiled rich kid having a driver and such a big house. Little did everyone know that I was actually the poor-no-house kid.

"We're here," he said suddenly and pulled to a stop in front of the club. I rolled my eyes at him but smiled. We would get along just fine. He started unbuckling his seatbelt to come and open my door, but I put my hand over his to stop him.

"I can get my own door."

"What time do you get off?" Garrett asked. I hesitated, not wanting to make him take me home so late.

"I get off at one. If it's too late for you, I can just get a cab." I was silently hoping it wouldn't be a big deal, since I didn't even know the address to Liam's house.

"No, it's not a big deal. I'll be right here at one," he said with a smile. With a "thank you" and a smile, I opened the door and stepped outside. With a wave to Garrett, I headed to the employee entrance. I knocked on the door three times, and it opened up to Tom standing there once again.

"Hey, Tom," I said, setting my bag on a hook.

"Hey, Jenna. Who did you wave to in that black car that dropped you off?" Tom asked, shutting the door.

"It was a friend," I said, which wasn't too big of a lie. "How long are you working?"

"Until eleven. I got a girl at home who needs some attention," he said, wiggling his eyebrows.

"Eww, that's disgusting," I said, scrunching up my nose. "Since I probably won't be seeing you before you get off, I wanted to tell you something," I said. I knew I just had to get this over with, quick like a Band-Aid. "Today is my last day."

I watched as his expression morphed into confusion.

"Why? You're not running off with some boyfriend, are you?"

"No, I'm not." I held back my laughter. "I'm actually going to go back home and…go to school," I lied. I knew I shouldn't have done that, and I hated that I had to. I just knew that if Tom knew about me and Liam's deal, he wouldn't be happy with me. Plus, he didn't know that I didn't have any parents or that I lived in New York by myself.

"Really? Good for you, kid!" He grinned at me as he walked over to hug me. "Be good, okay? Don't cause your parents too much trouble, and don't get in trouble at college. You're there to learn," Tom said sternly, pulling away and wagging his finger at me. I rolled my eyes.

"I will, *Dad*. Thank you, Tom, for everything you've done for me while I've been here. I'll miss you."

"I'll miss you too, Jenna. If you're ever back in New York, come by and say hi. I know Kendra would love to see ya."

"I will. Bye, Tommy." Before I could start crying, I hugged his big frame one last time before I left to go to work. *This is going to be a long night.*

Unfortunately, it was. From the moment I walked to the bar, I was swarmed with people yelling me their drink orders. The club was packed tonight, even though it was only Thursday. When the girls did their thing at the top of the hour, we still had people lining up for drinks. Although we were busy, time didn't seem to go by faster. Instead, it seemed to go slower. The clock was slowly inching its way to ten when finally people stopped coming up to the counter and us bartenders got a brief break. I knew Candy was off at eleven, so now was the best time to tell her. I was going to really miss working with her, because she seemed to get me. We both had been through hard times, totally different things, but it still brought us closer.

"Hey, Candy, can I talk to you for a moment?" I called over to her. She was on the other side of the bar, sent me a nod, and worked her way over to where I was in the corner, where I knew no one could hear us.

"What's up?"

"I wanted to tell you tonight is my last night. I know it's so sudden, and I wouldn't be doing it if I didn't need to." I stood there, waiting for her to blow up almost like Sophia had, but instead I saw her nod.

"You have to do what you have to do," she said, patting my arm. *Wait? What was that?*

"Wait. You're not mad at me or going to yell at me about why I'm leaving?" I was not expecting this reaction at all.

"No, because I trust that you are doing this for an important reason." I cringed inwardly at that. This was anything but important. "You just have to make sure to keep in touch with me and come see Sky every once in a while." I grinned at the mention of her four-year-old daughter.

"I promise I will. Oh, I finally got a cell phone, so add your number," I said, suddenly remembering I had it in my mini pocket. When I handed her my phone, she punched in her number before handing it back to me. I smiled sadly at her and pulled her into a hug.

"I'll miss you," I mumbled.

"Me too, Jenna. But we will stay in touch," she said firmly, pulling away from me. My eyes pooled with tears, but I forced them back. I wasn't going to cry. Unfortunately, our little moment got ruined as a guy came up to the bar wanting a drink. With a sigh from both of us, we got back to work.

When eleven hit, Candy said one last goodbye to me and made me promise to text her tomorrow before leaving. I looked after her, feeling sad, but at the same time happy. I was glad she wasn't mad at me nor did she push me to tell her why I am leaving. The rest of the night passed by quickly after that. Soon, I was walking up the stairs to Teddy's office to tell him I was leaving. With a deep breath, I knocked on the door and entered when he called for me to come in.

"Oh hello, Jenna. Is everything okay?" Teddy asked, gesturing for me to sit across from him.

"No, everything is okay," I answered, taking a seat. "I just came up here to tell you tonight is my last night here."

"Oh."

"I know it's sudden, and I am sorry for the inconvenience that it may cause, but I have some things I have to take care of for a while."

"You're not in trouble, are you? You can tell me." I smiled at him but shook my head. Knowing all these people cared for me made me feel warm inside. "Well, if you ever need anything, you can come to me. We'll miss you around here, but you gotta do what you gotta do."

"Thank you for understanding, Teddy," I said sincerely.

"It's no problem, hon. You can come by for your check next week, or I can give it to Candy."

"I'll come by in a week. Thank you again," I

said, standing up.

"Just take care of yourself. You're a great girl." He pulled me in for a hug, giving me a tight squeeze before letting me go. With my final goodbye, I nodded at him before leaving his office and heading back downstairs.

I wasn't all that close with any of the other workers, so I didn't stay and say goodbye. I didn't think I had another goodbye in me, to be honest. With a smile at the guard by the door, I nodded in thanks at him before stepping out into the cool night air. Before the door could shut, I took one last look at the club, saying a silent goodbye. When I turned around, I saw Garrett parked at the curb, where he said he would. Walking toward the car, I opened the passenger's side and got in.

"Thanks for picking me up."

"No problem. Home?" he asked. I could tell he was tired, so I nodded.

During the ride back, I leaned my head on the headrest, staring out the window as an Ed Sheeran song played softly in the background. As we passed cars and buildings, I couldn't help but wonder if I'd made a mistake.

Chapter Five

The next morning, I woke up to the sun shining on my face. I rolled over, covering my face with my pillow. When I got home last night, I found the house empty, not really to my surprise. I'd changed and slid into my new bed, but as I lay there, I couldn't fall asleep. I'd stared up at the ceiling, willing myself to sleep, but for some reason I couldn't. All night, I tossed and turned. Sleep finally overcame me around five this morning. I peeked open one eye and saw it was only nine. *I only got four hours of sleep!* Groaning, I laid my head back on the pillow, not wanting to get up.

The idea of having to get out of my comfy bed to face reality was not what I wanted. I wished I could just sit in bed all day and not worry about anything. In fact, I wished I could stay here for this entire year, only to leave it when my deal with Liam was done. If only it were that simple. After five minutes of protest, I finally got up and headed to shower. I hated that I was one of those people where if I was up, I was up. No going back to sleep for me. I turned on the big shower, letting the water warm up before stripping out of my PJs. You would think since I got up early almost every day I would be used to it, but nope. Instead, it seemed to get harder every day.

Stepping under the warm water, I closed the glass door behind me. As I tilted my face up, I let the water run down me, feeling all of the tension seep out of my body. I continued on washing my hair and body before reluctantly getting out. My fingers were pruned as I wrapped a fluffy baby blue towel around me. It was the softest towel I'd ever felt! With my blonde hair hanging down in my face and shoulders, I walked to the mirror.

The girl staring back at me was the same girl I'd seen for the past three years. I hadn't changed much since puberty hit or since I left high school. Only a few things were different: my blonde hair was longer, since I hadn't cut it since I left the home; my green eyes were duller with huge bags under them; and I looked a tad bit skinnier because I sometimes didn't get enough to eat. I guess I could be considered lucky I didn't gain the freshman fifteen that most do after graduating. Staring back at me was the same girl who had worked countless useless jobs for nothing and who hadn't had the easiest life. With a sigh at my reflection, I grabbed my brush and brushed my hair before leaving the bathroom to get dressed.

When I walked into my huge closet, I was struck again with how big and nice it was. As I got dressed, I wondered why people would need a closet so big. I slid on a pair of dark-wash skinny jeans, a cute maroon and grey quarter-sleeve shirt, and a pair of dark blue flats. I grabbed my cell phone and headed to get something to eat. I honestly didn't know why I even bothered to get dressed when I wouldn't be leaving the house, but whatever. *I guess I better ask Liam what I'll be doing, now that I don't work.* Walking into the kitchen, I froze mid-step as Liam sat at the bar drinking a cup of coffee and reading the paper. *What is he doing home? It's almost ten in the morning.* Not knowing if I should say good morning or not say anything at all, I walked toward the cabinet and grabbed a coffee mug, filling it up.

He was dressed in a black suit with a white button-up shirt and a dark blue tie. He must be getting ready to go to work, or he'd already been at work. I wasn't sure which. Liam didn't say anything as I moved around the kitchen, but I could feel his blue eyes following my every move. Gathering some courage, I turned and faced him, holding my cup against my chest, almost like a shield.

"So…" I started to say, "I quit my jobs."

"Good," Liam said in his smooth voice, no longer looking at me but down at the newspaper in front of him.

"Is there something you want me to do? Like clean the house or…" I trailed off, not knowing if he was even listening to me.

"No, I have a maid for that," was all he said. I couldn't help but glare at him. It was like talking to a wall, for crying out loud.

"Then what am I supposed to do?" I asked, trying to keep my anger at bay.

"I don't know. Keep yourself busy." He shrugged, then stood up and made his way over to me. I thought he was going to hug me or something, but instead, he pushed by me to put his cup in the sink. He walked past me again, out of the kitchen. I followed, wanting some answers to our little deal.

"Liam!" I called after him. "Are you going to leave me in the dark about our whole fake marriage?" I asked. It would be nice if I knew what to expect or something, anything.

"I already told you," he said, coming to a stop and turning to face me.

"No, you didn't. I need to know what is going to happen and what I have to do. I uprooted my entire life for you, Liam. The least you could do was answer some of my questions," I reasoned. He stared at me for a minute before sighing loudly, like I was ruining his day or something. He turned back around and walked into the living room. I took that as he was going to answer my questions, so I followed after him and sat down on one side of the couch while he sat in the chair. He looked at me expectantly, waiting for me to ask.

"What am I supposed to do, now that I don't work?" I asked first.

"I don't know. Read, write, workout, swim, go shopping," he said, sounding bored already. *Yeah, like I was going to go shopping every day for a year.* I almost snorted at that thought.

"Why did you want me to quit my jobs?"

"Look, I don't care what your situation is, whether you ran away from home because Daddy wouldn't give you what you wanted, or if you came to New York for some stupid dream that didn't happen. I do not honestly care. All that matters is that my parents like you and that we get married as soon as possible so I can get the business. After this year, I do not plan on seeing your face again." I stared at him, wide-eyed and hurt, as he stood up and walked away.

Liam didn't know anything about me, and it hurt that he made assumptions. *Why does everyone assume I'm some rich daddy's girl and will throw a fit if I don't get what I want?* I glared at the seat Liam had just been in, wishing he was still there so I could burn holes into his body with my eyes. I hated when people just assumed what I was like. Everyone judged a book by its cover, and they shouldn't. That book could be interesting, and maybe it'd gone through hard experiences. But they would never know. Maybe the outside cover was worn and weathered, but that didn't mean that the inside was same way. The pages could be in perfect condition or only slightly ripped and torn.

I heard a door slam shut down the hall, and I knew Liam had left. *Must have left through the garage.* The only place I hadn't seen yet. Taking a deep breath, I stood up, pushing my anger toward Liam down, and went to grab my coffee I left in the kitchen. I then headed to the garage. *Let's see what Liam's got in here.* I opened the door and walked out, turning on the light. I stared around the huge garage and at the expensive-looking cars. There were three sitting there, and there was an empty spot for the fourth, which Liam must have taken. The garage wasn't just for cars, though. On the left side were shelves that had what looked like tools and food storage. And on the right was a weird closet thing that held I didn't know what. Setting my mug on the counter right beside a sink, I walked toward the first car.

It was a deep grey color and kind of small. It looked to be a Porsche, sleek and fancy. Moving onto the one to the left of it, I ran my finger over the cherry-red paint of a Jeep. I couldn't help but stare in awe. I'd always wanted a Jeep. As I moved away from it, I glanced at it over my shoulder before heading to the last car down by the weird closet. It was a white Range Rover. It looked to be in the same great condition as the other two. *Wonder what car Liam took?* I wondered, looking at the empty spot.

Deciding I wanted to snoop, I opened the weird closet. Inside were boxes taped shut with no labels. Glancing around, making sure no one was really around, I reached for a box. *Wonder what he has in here.* The tape was loose, so I was able to get a fingernail under one side and pull it. I lifted the sides and peeked inside. Confused, I reached in and pulled out football trophies.

2007-2008 FOOTBALL CHAMPIONSHIP
LIAM STANFORD

Wow. *Liam played football?* I set that trophy back inside and opened the box further. The entire thing was filled with trophies and medals, but of different sports, such as baseball, football, and basketball. I let out a low whistle, impressed. I could almost see Liam playing sports, but the image of a cold businessman still stuck in my head. Putting that box away, I pulled out another one. This one was filled with pictures. I pulled one out, and I smiled down at a picture of Liam from when he looked to be only ten or so. He was holding a football under his arm and grinning at the camera, missing a tooth from his bottom and top jaw. His features were younger and rounder, his smile genuine. I set the picture down and pulled out another one. In this one, he looked a few years older, his brown hair floppy and long, hanging around his face. His face was sharper than in the picture from years before. He had a set of straight white teeth, which could be seen from him grinning at the camera. He gripped a basketball in his hand, holding out in front of his body. Liam looked happy, and his blue eyes were twinkling.

As I grabbed another photo, my grin got wider. This picture had to be from Liam's senior year. It was of him standing in a baseball uniform. He had a hat on, but I could tell his floppy long hair was gone, replaced with a shorter style. His shoulders were wider, and I could practically see his muscular arms through his shirt. His sharp, high cheekbones and jaw line replaced his rounder face from years before. There was black marker on his cheeks under his eyes. His feet were shoulder width apart, a baseball bat held between his hands across his shoulders and a mitt with a baseball at his feet. In this photo, he wasn't smiling. He was just looking hard at the camera.

I stared at the photo, amazed that he had done all three big sports in high school. As I set the photo back, I noticed multiple ring boxes under a pile of photos. Curious, I moved the photos and grabbed a dark green ring box and opened it. Inside laid a football championship ring. It was huge and had a green stone in the middle, and surrounding it was the word **"Football."** Shutting it, I grabbed a few more to open them. I got the same result, but with other sports. Liam had five rings total: two football, one basketball, and two baseball. *Goddamn.* They were all huge and nice looking. *Why are they packed away in a box outside?* If I had ones like these, I'd have them inside and maybe wear them from time to time.

Instead of going through the rest of the boxes, I put my current one away and shut the closet doors. Still thinking about the rings, photos, and trophies/medals, I grabbed my half-full coffee mug and headed back inside. I dumped my coffee out and leaned against the counter, biting my bottom lip in thought. If Liam was as good as those trophies and rings showed, then why wasn't he still playing? He's only twenty-four, not at all close to the age where he couldn't be playing a sport anymore, whether it be football, baseball or basketball. And how can the boy in those photos look so different then the man I see today? Did something happen?

I knew I wouldn't get any answers if I asked. Plus if I brought up anything about what I saw, he would know I'd gone snooping. Sighing, I let it go, but I knew I would be asking about them soon. Between looking in the garage and finding those things, that killed about thirty minutes of my time. I glanced around the kitchen and tapped my fingers

57

against the counter. It was only eleven and I was bored. *This is going to be a long-ass year.* With nothing to do, I figured I might as well check out the library for a while. With that thought in mind, I headed there. I was going to stop by my room to grab my phone, but with no one to call or text, I just left it there. No use in grabbing it, since I might end up leaving it in the library anyways.

As I walked into the library, I was again stunned at the room. It was basically a real library inside of a house. The walls were jammed with books. A big, comfy couch and chair sat off to the side, and a long table sat in the middle where you could work if needed. The little bit of wall I could see was painted a deep red, and the entire room screamed peace and home. I'd always loved the library, whether it was the school's or the one a few miles from the home. When I needed to just get away I always went there or the small bookstore, but that was usually too far for me to walk. A smile spread across my face as I slowly walked along one side of the room, running my fingers across the spines of books.

The scent of the room was a mix of old books, wood, and something else I couldn't place. Something about it made me feel at home and relaxed; this was definitely going to be my place in the entire house. I looked over the titles of books before they landed on a familiar one. Grabbing the spine, I pulled out George Orwell's *1984.* I'd read it in high school and somehow fell in love with it. Something about the story fascinated me and made me think about what if society was really like that. What would happen to us? Who would I be and what would I be doing? Would I be Winston and break the rules wanting to know the truth, or would I be Parson, who is ignorant of everything around him?

Grabbing the book, I made my way over to the comfy leather-looking chair and sat in it. I almost moaned as my body sunk into the couch and hugged it. The couch was really, really comfortable. With a content smile, I cracked open the book and got to reading. Everything around me faded. I was immersed inside the book, even though I'd read it multiple times. When reading, I let myself be taken in and surrounded by the book, like I was really inside of it. Reading was a way of letting everything fade away and be forgotten for a few moments. I didn't have to worry about making rent, my jobs, or now what I have to do with Liam's deal; everything just melted away and I was able to focus fully on the story and being one with it.

Hours passed as I read, ignorant of the time ticking by. I came to a stop at the end of a chapter, dog-earing the page, and set the book down to stretch my neck. My neck was now cramped and aching. When I stretched out my legs, popping noises could be heard as my stiff joints and muscles finally moved. When I looked down at the book, I realized I was more than halfway done. Holding my neck with my hand, I glanced at the clock before coming back to it. *Wow, I've been reading for almost five hours!* I stood up and stretched my back before my stomach started growling. Grabbing my book and placing it on the table, I left the library to make my way to the kitchen.

I walked funny the whole way there, feeling a little stiff from sitting down a long time. Heading into the kitchen, I grabbed a glass and filled it with water before gulping it all down in a matter of seconds. My stomach still growled, so I grabbed a random container from the fridge and microwaved it. Dinner was coming early today. Rolling my shoulders as I waited for my food, I wondered if Liam would be home tonight. *Probably not.* I wanted to talk to him, but with the way he'd acted earlier made me a little reluctant to. If he was just going to insult me again, I didn't want to talk to him.

If we did sit down and tried to get to know one another, things would be better. Maybe this deal wouldn't be so bad, but it seemed I was the only one who cared about that. I had no idea how we were going to convince his parents that we were in love. I hadn't even been in the same room as him for more than twenty minutes, and I knew nothing about him other than he played sports in high school. And I only knew that because I snooped around.

I sighed, and the microwave beeped. I dished the food out on a plate. Looked like tonight I was having stir fry. *I really need to buy actual food and make it myself.* I didn't know how much longer I could eat microwave food. I took a seat at the bar and ate my food by myself in silence. It wasn't like I wasn't used to eating alone. This place just made me feel even more alone, given its size. With my tiny apartment my presence took up space, so I didn't feel like it was just me, but here it was the opposite. I hadn't felt this lonely in a while.

As I was finishing up my food, I heard a door being opened and slammed shut, followed by a giggle. *Wait. Liam doesn't giggle.* With raised eyebrows, I stood up before going and peeking around the wall. Just a few feet from me was Liam, pushing some brunette against the wall while sucking or kissing her neck. I scrunched up my nose as I watched and heard the girl moan. From what I could see of the girl, she was pretty. With Liam covering most of her body, I could only make out that she was wearing a dress, and a small one at that. With his head buried in her neck, I could see her red lipstick smudged, and I knew it was all over Liam's face and neck.

Disgusted, I pulled my head back. Liam's little speech from when I'd first arrived ran through my head. *"If I bring women back here, I expect you to be in your room or leave. I don't want them asking questions."* For some reason, knowing Liam brought a woman here and that he was in a heated make-out session with her just down the hall made my chest ache. I guess I didn't think he was serious about bringing women here. Trying to be quiet, I grabbed my plate and set it in the sink. Guess I'd have to clean it tomorrow. I tip-toed over and peeked around down the hall. They were still there, and that was the only way to get to my room. *What am I going to do?*

Just as I thought about trying to head to the living room since it was closer, I heard Liam's voice.

"Come here." I peeked around the corner but

quickly retracted my head. They were coming this way! I pressed myself tightly against the wall, silently wishing I was invisible. I heard the girl's heels click against the tile floors, and I bit my lip as they got closer. From the corner of my eye I saw Liam come into view, then the girl he was with. I saw him glance at the kitchen so I pressed further into the wall, wanting to become one with it. I said a silent "thank you" for not turning on the light when I came down here to eat. Thankfully, they passed by the kitchen, and I heard their footsteps continue to the spiral stairs. I waited for his door to shut, but it never did.

Not caring or chancing Liam would come back this way, I ran to my bedroom, shutting the door. I leaned against it, breathing heavily. *Man, I need to work out.* I smiled a small smile, glad I didn't get caught. Who knows what would have happened if Liam had seen me? Taking a deep breath, I looked around the room, knowing I was going to be in here all night. I changed out of my clothes and into my PJs and washed my face. When I exited the bathroom, I froze when I heard a noise. *What the hell?* Confused, I looked around before silently opening my door an inch.

I could instantly hear moaning. Groaning and scrunching up my face in disgust, I shut my door, but I could still slightly hear it. *Does that woman have a microphone? I can hear her through the walls and downstairs! That's why Liam didn't close his door, to make sure I could hear him and stay away. Don't worry. I didn't plan on coming out.* Frowning, I climbed into bed, leaning against my pillow. When I heard the random girl's moans, I covered my ears and groaned loudly. It was going to be a *long* night.

Chapter Six

Somehow I fell asleep sometime during the night. I kept my mind off of the sounds coming through the walls by playing on my phone and looking up YouTube videos. The sound of voices woke me up, and I groaned loudly, pulling my pillow over my head. No way in hell was I going out there, especially with that girl Liam had over. I rolled over and stared up at the ceiling. It was Sunday, so it had only been a day living with Liam. I was already done.

This deal wasn't going to work. *Why did I even take it in the first place?* Yes, I needed the money, but I didn't think it was worth it. Liam was asking me to lie to his entire family, fake that I was in love with him, get married, and then leave when the year was up. Yes, I knew I should have thought about all that before agreeing, but hey, I didn't say I was smart. Hearing Liam and that girl having sex while I was only a floor away made me realize that this deal wasn't right, for anyone.

I didn't want to hurt and lie to people I hadn't

even met just so Liam could get the company from his father. I wasn't going to be some pawn in this little game. I still had my pride. Well, most of it anyways. I could still go back to my jobs and maybe hopefully my apartment. I just had to tell Liam I was not going to do this anymore and that I would be leaving. Nodding at myself and my decision, I pulled the covers away and got out of bed.

As I moved around my room, I heard what I thought was the front door open, then close. *Okay, now is my time.* I quickly went and washed my face before throwing on a pair of sweats and a loose t-shirt. There wasn't anyone here to impress, so why get dressed up? I walked out of my room, pulling my hair into a messy ponytail, and headed toward the kitchen. My footsteps were soft on the tile because of my socks. I glanced at the clock and saw it was only a quarter after nine. So early on a Sunday. Wanting to get this over with so I could run away like a dog with its tail stuck between its legs, I looked around for Liam.

I didn't find him in the kitchen, living room, or even his bedroom. I wondered where he could be. I didn't think he was the one who'd left earlier. With a quick glance in the garage, I realized I was correct because all four cars were parked. When I headed back to the kitchen, I could actually feel myself starting to worry. Stupid, I know. I heard a splashing noise and turned my head to look out the window. I could just make out a body moving in the pool. Found him.

Heading outside, I took a deep breath when I was

close enough to the pool. *Here we go. We can do this, Jenna.*

"Liam?" I called out. Thankfully, just as I called his name, his head popped up from the water at the other end of the pool. He jerked his head in my direction.

"Jenna?"

"I need to talk to you," I said as he worked his way toward me. He was only a few feet away from me when he stood up, the water coming to the middle of his thigh. I looked down his shirtless body, and my mouth dried up. The man worked out! Water rolled down his toned chest to his stomach, before his swim shorts soaked it up. A hard eight-pack graced his stomach, and my hands twitched, wanting to feel it. Without his dress shirt on, I realized his arms were bigger than I had originally thought. They were roped in muscle. He wasn't even flexing, and they stood out, well defined. Liam's brown hair stuck to his forehead, and drops of water hung at the tips. Seeing a man shirtless, with water dripping off of his body, made my body flush. The idea of running my tongue across his chest came to mind, and I didn't care that the liquid was chlorine and not regular water.

"Jenna?" Liam snapped his fingers in front of my face, and I jerked my gaze away from his body. My face flushed. I cleared my throat, feeling embarrassed for being caught staring at him.

"Oh, sorry. I, um..." I tried to remember why I came out here in the first place, but my mind was blank. Liam smirked at me as he walked up the steps, eventually stepping out of the pool. Without meaning to, I looked over his body again, wanting to run my hands down his wet front. *Jenna, stop! You came out here for a reason, and that reason isn't to eye-rape him.* "I need to talk to you about our deal," I finally forced myself to say. If you were in my position, you would understand how hard it would be to say something while looking at a hot, shirtless guy.

"Again?" Liam asked, grabbing a towel and running it across his head.

"Yes. I...I can't do it." He turned and stared at me. "After hearing you and that girl, I know I can't do this. I can't be a pawn in your game."

"You think you can just walk away?" Liam said, dropping the towel at his feet and taking a step toward me. I gulped and took a small step backwards. I couldn't go far because the pool was right behind me.

"Yes...and I will." I pushed down my nervousness and straightened my back. "You are just using me to get the company from your father. I won't be used then cast aside."

"Jenna, you chose this. You could have said no, but you didn't. You also signed a contract that is non-negotiable." He stood right in front of me, staring down. With his huge frame surrounding me, I felt really intimidated.

"I don't care about the contract or the money anymore. I just want to leave. You can find another girl to use," I bit out, feeling anger rise inside of me.

"Wow, you really are stupid. The contract you signed states that you are not allowed to get out of it until the year is up, or if you do, you owe *me* one million dollars." *What?! Damn it. I knew I should have read that contract in detail.* He did that on purpose because he knew I didn't have any money. I'd have to stay here. I glared at him.

"You know I don't have that kind of money."

"Yes, I do. That is why the contract is the way it is. You will stay here with me for a year, whether you want to or not," he hissed at me before turning and walking away. I stomped my foot on the ground like a little kid, but I was too angry to care at the moment. Liam had cornered me, and I stupidly fell for it! Now I was really stuck here until the end. Liam's figure disappeared inside the house. I let loose a string of curse words.

I really was stupid. I should not have taken this deal. I should not have trusted Liam with that contract, and I should have known this was too good to be true. I was mad at Liam, but I was mostly mad at myself for actually thinking this deal wouldn't be a terrible thing. My anger simmering down, I walked down to the bungalow and sat on the bench. *I hate my life.*

The rest of the day passed by slowly. I spent a good three hours outside just thinking and yelling at myself. It seemed Liam had no plans of leaving the house, so when I walked back inside, he was eating in the kitchen. I passed him, not saying a word, and headed to my bedroom. I spent the rest of the day/night avoiding him. When I ventured out of my room a few hours later to grab some dinner, I saw a light down the hall on and knew Liam was in his office. Not caring if I was quiet or not, I grabbed a container of food and microwaved it before heading back to my room to eat. The less time I spent around Liam, the better.

When I woke up on Monday morning, Liam was already gone, and I was thankful. This was going to be the longest year of my entire life, but I was determined not to let Liam get to me. If he wanted a wife, he was going to get one. Two could play at this game. I had no problem spending his money, changing his house, or acting like the spoiled brat he seemed to think I was. He should have picked another girl to use.

The rest of Monday I walked around the house, coming up with ideas on how to change it. If I was going to be here, it was going to look different, more homey. Right now it was empty and cold. All week I was going to redecorate to keep myself busy.

Dinner came and went, and still no Liam. I grabbed a blanket from my bedroom and headed to the living room to watch a movie. Going over to the wall with movies lined up in every space available, I ran my eyes across each shelf, trying to find a good movie. For someone who wasn't ever home, he sure did have a lot of movies.

Finally I grabbed the movie *Dear John* and then got to work trying to figure out his DVD and sound system. Yes, even Liam had Nicholas Sparks movies. It took me five minutes just to turn it on. When I got the movie in, I jumped back onto the couch with the remote and curled up in my blanket. The entire time I watched it, I couldn't help but wonder if I'd ever get a love like Savannah and John's. Probably not after this, honestly. Of course, me being a girl, I cried throughout the movie, wanting a love like theirs. When it ended, it was only nine, so I put in another movie, something less sad. When the credits started rolling for *21 Jump Street*, I got up and headed to see if Liam had popcorn. I found some in only a couple of minutes before I was back on the couch clicking "Play" and eating.

As I watched the movie, laughing every so often, I could feel my eyes starting to droop. The popcorn bowl sat on the coffee table, completely empty. The harder I tried to stay awake, the more my eyes wanted to shut. I lost the fight a few minutes later and let sleep take me.

***

Liam

I glanced at clock on the dashboard and saw it was nearing midnight. I looked back at the road, thinking about Jenna. She should be asleep by now, so I didn't have to worry about seeing her. I thought back to when I first saw her at Tammy's club.

Friday, two weeks ago
She was standing behind the bar in a tank top that was tight and fit her like a glove. From my seat in the dark corner, I couldn't make out her eyes, but I bet they were a pretty blue color. Her blonde hair was in a ponytail, and she moved around the bar with ease. I could tell she had been working here for a while and knew her way around.
I watched as a man came up to her and started

flirting. I found it amusing, as she shot down whatever he was saying. She wasn't even giving him the time of day. Something about her intrigued me. I couldn't help but wonder what she was doing in a place like this. She's probably trying to show her daddy that she's fine without his money. *She might be perfect for what I had in mind.*

My father thought that if I settled down, I would be better qualified to take over the business. Yeah, right. Just because I was not married didn't mean I didn't know how to run a company. My father said the other day that he would step down in a few months, and if I wanted his position, then I'd better show him I was more mature than I used to be. I made the mistake of telling him I was in a "serious" relationship. So now he wanted to meet her as soon as possible. I needed to find the perfect woman to convince him. I couldn't bring my usual type, because that wouldn't show my father anything. That was why I was here, scouting out women to see if they would work.

"Hello. Can you ask that girl over there to bring me a drink?" *I asked a waitress who was about to pass by. She looked at me, confused, but nodded and headed back to the bar. I watched as she went around and told the girl I'd been eyeing to bring me my drink.*

She stepped around the bar, and I felt my pants tighten. She was wearing a pair of shorts that didn't cover much, showing off her long legs. Her tight tank top had risen up, showing an inch of skin below her belly button. She was hot. I could give her that. I watched as she looked around until she

71

came close enough to me and stopped. Now that she was up close I saw her eyes were a light green, instead of the blue I'd originally thought. She stared at me, frozen, her green eyes trailing across my face. I tried not to smirk at her reaction.

"Here you go," she all but whispered before turning and walking away. I watched after her, narrowing my eyes as I stared at her little ass encased in those booty shorts. Nice ass. I took a sip of my whiskey. There was something different about her. I knew she was the one I needed. She seemed like the type my parents wouldn't expect me to be with.

I sat at the table, watching her for another hour or so before she looked like she was about to leave. Standing up, I dropped a twenty on the table, buttoned up my suit jacket, and made my way out the door. I was going to talk to her. I got in my car, waiting for her to appear so I could discuss a deal with her. A few minutes later she appeared, sending a wave behind her, then heading in my direction. She had her arms wrapped around herself, and she had a small, thin jacket on. She must be cold. As she walked by, I told my driver to pull up next to her. I watched as she looked around nervously and froze as my car came to a stop beside her. I stepped out. Her green eyes widened at my appearance.

"I need you to come with me," I said.

"W-what?" she stuttered out, obviously confused.

"I need you to come with me," I said slowly. Did she not hear me?

"Excuse me? I am not going anywhere with you.

72

I have no idea who you are. And don't talk down to me as if I'm stupid or a child," she said, narrowing her gorgeous green eyes at me. I clenched my jaw as she crossed her arms across her chest, staring at me stubbornly.

"Jenna, I need you to come with me. I have something to discuss with you." She looked at me like how the hell did I know her name? *"I was at the club, remember?"* I watched her as she had some internal debate. *"Jenna, I promise you I will not harm you. All I want to do is talk to you for a few minutes. Then I'll bring you back home."*

"Are you a rapist?" she finally asked after a few minutes of silence.

"No." I tried not to roll my eyes at her.

"Are you a killer?"

"No."

"I will only get in the car if you tell me your name."

"Liam, Liam Stanford." I waited to see if she would recognize me, but surprisingly, she didn't. I stepped aside and gestured to the car door. Hearing her sigh, I smiled inwardly and opened the door for her. Once I was in, I waved my driver forward and watched Jenna out of the corner of my eye. She was leaning against the door, trying to stay as far away as possible. About ten minutes later, the car came to a stop and I got out, waiting for Jenna. I figured since it was late and cold, we could talk over some coffee. Opening the front door to Starbucks, I waited impatiently for Jenna to notice. When we finally got inside, she went straight to the counter, which had a very bored barista behind it. After

hearing her order, I walked up behind her and purposely stood close by, telling the girl my order.

I noticed when she pushed her chest out toward me, but I ignored her as I paid. I walked to a table, glad no one else was here at this time of night; I wasn't surprised this place was open at 11:30. It was New York, after all. A few minutes later, the barista girl came and brought us our drinks and left, but not before practically pushing her breasts into my face. Normally I would go for it, but not today or with someone so young.

"So, what did you want to talk to me about?" Jenna finally asked, taking a sip of her drink.

"I want you to be my wife," I stated bluntly. Better to get straight to the point. I watched as she choked on her drink.

"W-What did you just say?" she choked out.

"I want you to be my wife." I took a sip of my coffee and leaned back, watching her. It wasn't that hard to understand. The air suddenly rang with Jenna's laughter. "Why are you laughing?" I bit out.

"Because you're joking." When I didn't agree that I was, she fell silent. "Are you being serious? We don't even know each other! Hell, I just met you minutes ago!" she yelled.

"Keep it down!" I hissed. I didn't want anybody else to know about this. It was going to stay between the two of us.

"How can you ask me that after you just practically proposed to me?" she replied. "You have to be joking right now, Liam. I am not going to marry you!"

"Yes, you will. I am not asking you to be my wife forever. I am asking you to be my wife for a year. Nothing more, nothing less." I only needed her so my parents could get to know her. Then, when I took the business, she would be gone. I couldn't care less where she went after that. I explained to her why I needed her and what she would get afterwards. I could tell she was really thinking about it, and I grinned mentally.

After dropping her off at her apartment, I knew she would say yes. This place was a dive and in a terrible part of town. A part of me wanted to make her say yes right now so I could get her out of this place faster, but I didn't. She needed to make this decision on her own. Driving back home, I leaned back in my seat and rubbed my forehead, feeling a headache coming on. I knew if she took the deal, she was going to make it harder than it needed to be.

I pulled into the garage and sighed. I was right. Jenna was making this harder than it needed to be. She didn't seem to get I was only doing this because I had to, not because I wanted to be with her. During the last few nights, I'd purposely stayed away from the house because I didn't want to get questioned. I didn't have everything figured out yet, and I couldn't answer her questions.

Yes, last night shouldn't have happened. I shouldn't have brought Breanna over and slept with her with Jenna in the house. But, at the time, I wanted Jenna to know I wasn't going to be all cuddly and nice when I didn't have to be. This deal was strictly professional. It didn't help though, when she would look at me with those piercing green eyes of hers or when she smiled. I wouldn't ever admit it out loud, but her stubbornness was refreshing. I liked that she argued with me.

Shaking my head at myself, I walked into the house. I would not fall for Jenna, I promised myself. As I walked down the hall, I heard music and saw light coming from the living room. Frowning, I walked toward the living room and saw credits rolling for a movie. I didn't see Jenna asleep on the couch until the light from the TV flashed across her face. Her long eyelashes framed her cheeks, and her pink lips were curved into a smile like she was having a good dream. Staring at her sleeping made something ache inside of my chest.

I glanced at the clock and saw it read 12:30. As gently as I could, I slid my hands under her butt and her upper back. I lifted her up and carried her toward her room. I felt her move in my arms, and I froze but relaxed a second later as she snuggled deeper in my chest. I softly laid her on the bed, pulling the blanket off of her sleeping form and placing the covers on top of her. I brushed a stray blonde piece of hair away from her face and smiled softly at her. I had only known her for a week, but she already had a small hold on me.

"Goodnight, Jenna," I whispered softly down at her before making my way out of her door, shutting it softly, then heading to my room.

Chapter Seven

Jenna

"But, Mommy, I want to go with you!" my five-year-old self said. My little hands were on her wrist, trying to pull her back toward me. Her blonde hair fell around her face as she knelt in front of me. Her green eyes stared into mine, and I tried not to cry. It was dark, and I was tired. I wanted to go back to bed.

"Honey, I will be back soon. I just need you to stay right here until I get back," she said, putting her hands on my little shoulders.

"I don't want to stay here," I whined again, holding my teddy bear in one hand and her arm in another.

"Jenna. Be a good girl and listen to Mommy," my mom said sternly. Her soft tone was replaced with something else. She had been doing that a lot lately, being nice one second, then being cold and rude the next. It wasn't always directed toward me, but these last two days it had been. I looked down at *the ground and nodded softly. I would always listen to Mommy. "I want you to know I love you, Jenna. I'll be back soon." She stood up and laid a quick kiss to my forehead. Giving me one last look, she turned and walked away, leaving me on the doorstep of some house.*

I watched her go, clenching my teddy bear tightly against my chest as tears rolled down my chubby cheeks. Even though I was only five, I somehow knew she wasn't going to come back. I watched her until I couldn't see her anymore. I sat down on the steps and stared in the direction she'd gone. Hours passed, and soon the sun started to come up. My tears had stopped and dried on my cheeks, my eyes drooping shut every minute, but I would force them open in case my mommy came back. Mommy will be back. *I sat there, waiting to see her tall figure come around the corner.*

I woke up with a start and felt tears rolling down my cheeks. I wiped them away, feeling my chest ache. I hadn't had that dream in a while. I used to quite often when I was younger, but over the years it disappeared. With a soft sigh, I slumped back in my bed. *Wait? I'm in my bed?* I jerked up and looked around my room. *I don't remember coming in here last night.* I remembered watching a movie and falling asleep on the couch, not here. Confused, I got out of bed and walked out of my room, oblivious to how my hair looked and that I was only in my PJs.

Surprisingly, Liam was sitting in the kitchen, drinking a cup of coffee and eating what looked like eggs. I saw it was only seven in the morning. I headed to the coffee machine, in dire need of some. My head hurt and my eyes ached. It felt like I'd cried in my sleep.

"Good morning," Liam said from behind me, surprising me. I almost spilled the coffee I was pouring.

"Morning," I croaked out, my throat dry. I brought my cup to my lips and took a quick gulp, wetting my mouth and needing the caffeine.

"Did you sleep okay?" I was really surprised that he was talking to me, but not wanting him to stop, I turned around.

"I did, thank you. Did you help put me in my bed last night?" I asked, leaning against the counter in front of him. He looked up, and I saw him look over my attire, then back to my eyes.

"I did. I came home late and found you asleep on the couch. Thought you would be more comfortable in your own bed." As he talked, I couldn't help but like the way his voice sounded. It was kind of deep but smooth and seemed to wash over me like water. *Wonder what his morning voice sounds like?*

Shaking the thought away, I replied, "Thank you, my bed is a lot more comfortable than the couch." I sent him a smile, to which he nodded. Hey, it was progress.

"I hired an assistant for you," Liam said a minute later. I raised my eyebrow at that. I needed an assistant? He must have seen the look on my face. "She's not really an assistant. More of a, what do you girls call it...makeup fashion person." He waved his hand around. I bit back a grin at his words. "She'll help you pick out clothes, do your makeup for special occasions, and later help with your schedule."

"My schedule?"

"Yes. When we come out with our engagement, people are going to want to see you and meet with you. You're going to have to be a social elite. Being a Stanford, you have to attend events and become involved in certain activities." The idea of having to become a social elite didn't sound so good. I didn't want to go to parties and talk to snooty rich people. Just the thought of it made me want to crawl into a hole and stay there.

"I have to?" I asked, giving him my puppy dog eyes.

"Yes, you will. And nope, puppy dog eyes don't work on me," he said, standing up and gathering his plates. *Damn it.*

"Fine," I said defensively. "What is my assistant's name?"

"Lennon Anderson. She will be here around nine, and she will be taking you shopping for some clothes. This Saturday we are going to my parents' so they can meet you."

"Isn't that a little too soon?" I asked. I wasn't ready to start meet his family and immediately start lying to them.

"No. My mother keeps pestering me about meeting you, and so does my sister," Liam said, setting his dishes in the sink. "I am thinking tomorrow we will go out and get a ring."

"A ring?"

"Did you hit your head last night? Yes, an

engagement ring, Jenna." Oh, right. It was way too early for this much information.

"Right. I knew that," I said, sending him a sheepish smile.

"I have to go to work. Let me know when Lennon gets here." He nodded at me, then left. I stared after him, trying to absorb everything he'd just told me. I had an assistant, I was getting an engagement ring tomorrow, and Saturday I had to meet Liam's parents. Wow, I could easily freak out right now. And, on top of that, Liam had an actual conversation with me.

With everything running through my mind, I headed back to my room to get ready before Lennon arrived. I spent the next two hours taking my time to get ready. I showered, shaved, made my bed, did my dishes as well as Liam's, and got dressed. I slipped on a pair of dark blue skinny jeans and a thin teal-colored sweater. I would like to say I have pretty good style, but not having much money, I usually just bought cheap items. Most of my clothes were really worn and/or came from the Salvation Army. I guess by having an assistant dressing me and having money, my style would get better.

Right as my butt hit the couch, the sound of knocking on the front door had me right back up again. I unlocked the door and opened it up, revealing a short, pretty, dark-haired girl. Her hair was dark brown and went past her upper back. Her skin looked porcelain, but with an olive tone. I knew she must have a mixed heritage. Staring up at me was a pair of pretty brown, almost hazel eyes.

"Hi, you must be Jenna. I'm Lennon!" She

beamed at me, sticking her hand out to shake mine.

"Oh, hi, yes, that's me. Nice to meet you." I shook her hand and stepped back. "Come in." I followed her to the living room, and she jumped onto the couch.

"So what did Liam tell you about me as your 'assistant'?" she asked, looking at me.

"Um, just that you'd be picking my outfits and helping me get ready for events, then my schedule later on. That's about it." I was surprised she called Liam by his first name, honestly.

"Of course, that sounds like Liam," Lennon said, rolling her eyes. She must have seen my confused look. "I grew up with him." Oh, that made sense. She didn't look to be twenty-four, though.

"Ohhh."

"I can tell from that tone that you don't really like him?"

"No, I do. He's just…" I tried searching for the right word.

"Confusing? Cold? Shuts everyone out? Yeah, I know what you mean. But once you get to know him, he's the greatest person you could ever meet." She smiled at me. When she talked about Liam, I could tell they had history together. Whether it was romantic or just friendship, I didn't know. "And I want you to know I know about the deal. I didn't want you to worry about that around me." That was one less person I had to lie to. "Anyways, ready to go shopping? We are going to make you look sexy."

I couldn't help but grin. There was something about Lennon I liked. I don't know if it was her carefree vibe or her slight quirkiness. I knew I would like her, even if I had only just met her two seconds ago.

"Okay, let me call Garrett to come around," I said, grabbing my phone.

"Hey, Jenna. What can I do you for?"

"Would it be okay if you came and picked me up? Lennon, my new assistant, is taking me shopping."

"Sure, no problem. Be there in just a minute." With that, he hung up.

"He'll be here in a minute. What are we going shopping for?" I asked.

"Everything! We need to get you dresses, skirts, blouses, heels, makeup," she rattled off. I stared at her as she listed off what we needed to do today. Well, good thing we were starting a little after nine or we wouldn't be finished by tonight. "I know it's a lot to take in, but don't worry. I will prep you with everything you will need to know. And you'll look great while doing so." She grinned at me cheekily.

I quickly went back to my room to grab my bag before meeting Lennon at the front door, which was open. She was talking to Garrett.

"Hey," I said, interrupting their conversation.

"Hey, Jenna. Ready to go shopping?" Garrett asked, his voice changing to a high pitch at the word "shopping."

"OMG yes!" I said back in the same annoying, high-pitched voice. Beside me, Lennon laughed, and he chuckled.

"Well, right this way, m'lady." He stepped back and gestured toward the car. Lennon and I slid into the back seat as Garrett started the car and drove down the driveway. "So, Oak Ridge Mall?" Lennon answered for me, since I didn't know.

"This mall has the best stuff. It's a little pricy, but that's not a problem," she said, waving her hand.

"Can't I just get some new pairs of jeans and a few shirts?" I asked. I really didn't like dressing up at all.

"No can do. Liam talked to me and said I can only let you get 'fancy' clothing. His words, not mine."

I guess I couldn't say I hated shopping, since I'd never done it extensively, but the sound of going to thousands of stores to try on stuff didn't seem fun to me.

"Come on, Jenna, doesn't shopping for hours sound like a blast?" Garrett asked in a high-pitched voice again as he looked at me in the review mirror.

"Very fun," I replied sarcastically.

"It's going to be fun, don't worry," Lennon said. *Yeah, right.* We pulled up to the entrance of the mall, and Lennon got out.

"Do you want to tag along, or do you want me to call you when we are finished?" I offered to Garrett.

"Shopping with two girls...I'll come and pick you guys up later. I have to keep my masculinity intact, but have fun," he said, shaking his head.

"I'll try. Call you later." With that, I got out of the car and shut the door before following Lennon inside the huge mall.

For the next couple of hours, we went to a ton of different stores, trying on practically everything they had. I stopped counting how many times I had been inside a dressing room.

I was carrying about six bags that were full of clothes, and Lennon said we still had a few more stores to go to. So far shopping hadn't been too bad, actually. Lennon was fun to hang out with, and there were a few times where I was almost on the floor laughing from her stories.

I learned about a little bit of her childhood with Liam and another guy named Blake. Apparently they all met when they were in seventh grade. Lennon had moved here from New Hampshire in the middle of the school year. Liam and Blake were already best friends, since their parents were friends, so when Lennon was getting picked on by some kids, they came to her rescue and they had been friends ever since, along with Liam's sister, Julie.

When I asked about Blake, I watched as her eyes glazed over when she described him. He was apparently tall, with short blonde hair and blue eyes. He was also muscular and apparently went to the gym on a regular basis. Blake worked at his father's construction company. They built everything from hotels to apartment buildings, even most of Liam's hotels. As Lennon described him, I knew she had a crush on her best friend. I hadn't met the guy, but I already knew I would like him.

I also learned that Lennon was a professional stylist/makeup artist. She had done everything from makeup for actors and actresses to Victoria's Secret models. Right now she had a small vacation, so she'd agreed to be my stylist for a while. As we walked into "one last store," which were Lennon's words even though she'd said that the last three stores, she turned to me.

"I don't want to intrude on your personal life or anything, but what made you take that deal of Liam's? I still can't believe he's stooped so low to take over his father's business," she asked, leafing through the rack of clothes.

"Well, I…I have some money issues, and I know it wasn't that best decision I have ever made, but the deal sounded good at the time. I never really thought of what I would have to do or what would be expected of me. I don't know what I was thinking at the time, agreeing to be his wife," I admitted. "It has only been five or six days, and I already regret it."

"What do your parents think of all this? Do they even know you're going to be marrying a stranger?"

I thought of my mother and sighed inwardly. I didn't know what she would say if she were here. I bet she wouldn't be proud of what I was doing, but I didn't really have a choice. I had no money, I'd been working two low-end jobs, and I'd been living in a shitty apartment in the shitty part of town.

"They aren't here anymore," I said, not wanting to get into it. I knew the moment I told her that my mom left me, she would pity me, and I hated when people did that. "I don't really like talking about it."

"Oh, I am so sorry," she immediately apologized.

"Don't worry about it. Most don't know."

"Does Liam?" I thought about it and shook my head. I didn't think he did, honestly. He probably still thought I was some rich spoiled girl that needed money since her dad wouldn't give her any.

"So does anyone else know about Liam and my deal?" I asked, changing the subject.

"Um, well, there's me, Liam, Blake doesn't know...yet. I don't think anybody else," she said.

"I told Garrett and my one friend at my old job, but that's it."

"You know no one else can know, right? If Liam's parents find out, then Liam is going to be super pissed. I know I don't know much about this deal between you guys, and I only just met you, but I don't want you getting hurt. This deal is bound to hurt someone, and that may be you. I know Liam is my best friend, but when it comes to women, he is not the greatest." She looked at me sadly.

I already knew I couldn't tell anyone about Liam and me and that we would have to come up with a story about how we met. And I figured Liam was a womanizer when he'd brought that random girl home. The more I thought about this, the more I realized I was a fucking idiot. Nothing good was going to come out of this whole ordeal.

"Jenna, don't worry. I mean, things could turn out different than what we think. Plus, I will be here to help you along the way, with Liam and everything else." She sent me a smile, and I smiled back at her. Well, at least I would have someone.

Two stores later, Lennon said we were done, and I almost kissed her right then and there. I called Garrett to pick us up and followed her outside, my arms heavy with bags. It was three in the afternoon, and we'd started at nine that morning. I was more than ready to be done. I had gotten seven dresses, all fancy ones for events, and matching high heels for all of them. Lennon wouldn't let me get anything lower than four inches. I got a lot of new tops and even some new jeans that Lennon said "were in style." Most of the stuff I was carrying was picked by her. I only got a few things I really wanted, like the jeans since they fit me perfectly. Lennon even made me buy a shitload of makeup so she wouldn't have to use her own on me.

As we piled everything into the trunk of the car, I only felt slightly bad for how much we had spent on everything. When I saw the price tag of the first dress, I almost fainted and told Lennon there was no way I was going to get it. All she did was pull out a black card and wave off my protests, saying Liam had given her permission to buy whatever I needed at no expense. Spending some of Liam's money didn't make me feel so bad. This was his whole idea anyways.

"Have fun shopping, you two?" Garrett asked as he drove away from the mall.

"Actually, yeah," I said. He turned his head and looked at me, surprised. I was surprised myself that I'd enjoyed it a little bit.

"See, told you it would be fun," Lennon said, grinning widely as she leaned back in the seat. I rolled my eyes inwardly but turned to her.

"Thank you for taking me shopping, Lennon. It was nice doing something somewhat normal."

"No problem. I don't mind."

On the ride home, all three of us talked about random topics before we pulled up the driveway. Garrett helped Lennon, and I grabbed my bags from the back before heading inside.

"God, woman, what did you get? Do you have the entire mall in these?" Garrett asked, his arms full of bags.

"Oh shut up," Lennon replied. As soon as I got the door open, we all trudged in before dropping the bags in the living room.

"Thank you, Garrett. You can go home. I don't plan on leaving again." I sent him a smile. He nodded and said goodbye to both of us before leaving.

"Thanks again, Lennon," another voice said from behind me.

"Hey, Lennon," Liam said.

"Hey." She went over to him and hugged him. I stared at them with wide eyes. I hadn't heard nor seen Liam so informal since I'd first met him. He always spoke formally, and I didn't think I had ever seen him smile like that before. His face was relaxed. "What are you doing here? I thought you were at work all day."

"I had a few things to talk about with Jenna," he said, looking over at me. Just a glance in my direction and his facial expression seemed to change. It seemed just the thought of me made him go sour. I looked down at the ground, hating the way he looked at me.

"I'd better get going then. See you later, Liam." I looked up just in time to see her kiss him on the cheek and give him a hug. A flash of jealousy ran through me at the sight of them. For some unknown reason, I wanted to know what it was like to be hugged by Liam. His strong arms wrapped around me would probably make me feel safe. "Bye, Jenna. Thanks for all the fun today. I'll text you later." She came over and surprised me by giving me a hug before leaving. I stood there, shocked. It'd been so long since I'd been really hugged that it was weird. There had only been three people I had hugged in the last few years, and they were Sophia, Candy, and Tom from work. They didn't really count, though.

"Jenna." Liam jerked me out of my thoughts.

"Yeah?"

"Are you ready to go?" he asked. I stared at him, confused.

"What?"

"Did you not hear what I said?" He rolled his eyes at me. "I said we need to leave and pick out a ring."

"I thought we were doing that tomorrow?"

"We were, but not anymore. Instead of meeting my parents on Saturday, we are meeting them tomorrow."

Hot man say what?

Chapter Eight

I stared at Liam, frozen. In less than twenty-four hours, I would be meeting his family for the first time and pretending I was deeply in love with him. I didn't think I could do this. No, I couldn't do this. As I stood there almost hyperventilating, a voice in the back of my mind started talking.

Jenna, it doesn't matter if you can't do this. You are going to have to. You got yourself into this mess, and you're going to have to get out of it yourself. This is not about you anymore. You are going to suck it up, stop whining, realize this is happening, and deal with it. From now on you are going to have to fake that you're in love and happy with Liam. Stop acting like a little girl.

I realized that the voice was right. My time of whining and thinking about how stupid I was to take the deal was over. It had happened, and I was going to have to deal with it. Time to start acting mature and not like some high school teenaged girl. I could do this.

"Yes, I'm ready," I said, swallowing and tilting

my head up. With a nod to Liam that I had everything I needed, I walked past him toward the garage. It took a minute before I heard his footsteps following me. Walking out to the garage, I stood off to the side waiting for him to grab the keys.

Without saying anything, he grabbed a random set hanging by the door before walking over to the Audi that hadn't been here the last time I was in the garage. I stood there gawking at it while Liam was already inside the driver's seat, obviously waiting impatiently for me. I quickly walked to the passenger's side and slid into the dark grey leather seat. The inside of the car was just as sleek as the outside.

Dark grey leather graced the seats, and the dashboard was black and smooth. There was a touch screen stereo system that could also hook to a phone. Clicking my seatbelt on, I ran my fingertips across the dash. This car probably cost more than my life and everything I own, doubled. I'd always loved cars, and even in high school I took an auto class all four years. It was by far my favorite class. Learning what made a car tick fascinated me for some reason. To me it was easier figuring out what was wrong with the car and fixing it, rather than communicating with people. Cars were simple. People were not.

Liam backed out of the garage, and soon we were flying down the driveway onto the road. Surprised at first at the speed we were going, I gripped the door handle, but after a minute, I let go and relaxed into the comfortable seat. Going fast didn't bother me. It made me feel free, like nothing could touch me.

As we came closer into town, Liam slowed the car and weaved around others. I watched as we passed by tall buildings and cute little shops lining the street. People dressed in suits and pant suits walked briskly past one another, either heading home or back to work. I noticed a few tourists as they walked slowly on the sidewalk, pointing at things.

A minute later, Liam pulled up in front of a building. Opening my door, I stepped out and gasped at the building. Tiffany and Co. *I'm getting a ring at Tiffany's?* A hand on my lower back brought me back to reality, and I turned to see Liam next to me. I leaned away from him, but his hand wrapped around my waist, pulling me to his side.

"Don't. We are out in public," he hissed down at me. Swallowing hard, I nodded and stepped back into his side. He opened the door and pushed me inside, following after me.

The moment I stepped inside, I felt like I had died. Cases upon cases were filled with diamonds. Multiple people stood around dressed in black, holding their hands in front of them, waiting to help someone. Just standing at the entrance made me feel so small and dirty compared to this place. I never thought I would ever be able to come to a place like this. It was every girl's dream to get a ring at Tiffany's, even a poor girl like me who never would be able to afford one in a million years.

"Mr. Stanford?" a female voice asked. I looked away from the cases of rings to the right of me. A woman stood there. She was middle aged, with brown hair to her shoulders. Her brown eyes were staring at Liam in shock.

"Hello. I'm here to pick out a ring with my fiancé," Liam said, his arm tightening around me. The lady turned her gaze to me, and I felt her scrutinizing me, like an ant beneath her feet. I watched as her brown eyes narrowed at me before turning back to Liam and sending him a wide grin.

"Of course, Mr. Stanford. I'm Karen. I'll show you what we have. "As she turned to lead us somewhere, I glanced down at my outfit and couldn't help but wonder what was wrong with it. A big hand wrapped around my wrist and pulled me along. I looked up just in time before I hit Liam's back. He looked down at me and clenched his jaw before turning back to Karen. *God, what is up with everyone today?*

Even though it was 4:30, the place was still busy as we weaved around people. We passed by a case, and my eyes widened at how huge the diamonds were on just one ring.

"Mr. Stanford, here are our finest rings. We have white gold, gold, silver, and platinum bands. We can provide any cut of diamond you want, as well as color." I stood to the side of Liam and watched as Karen pulled out cases filled with different types of rings. I stared down at them, not having known there was so many different rings to choose from. Who knew you could get pink, yellow, blue, and even green diamonds?

"Honey, go ahead and take a look," Liam said. His term of endearment surprised me, but I didn't show it. I sent him a fake smile and stepped away from him, closer to the rings. I felt both of their stares on me but ignored them as I excitedly looked from one ring to another.

There were so many to choose from that someone could easily become overwhelmed. As I looked at the ones in front of me, I didn't see any that popped out at me. Sure, they were beyond gorgeous, with big diamonds centered in the middle and little ones around the band. There were round, princess, oval, pear, emerald, heart, and square cuts. I could tell the lady was getting impatient, which was stupid for a sales person, so I pointed at one.

"Can I see that one?" I asked politely. I didn't know if I was allowed to just grab one. She nodded and handed me a pretty ring, its band silver with a few diamonds near the top and a big circle diamond in the center. I slid it onto my ring finger and looked down at it. It was obviously too big for my little finger and kept sliding down. *You know what? This is going to be my only wedding, so I might as well pick a ring I really want and like. Maybe at the end of the year Liam will let me keep it.*

"Here," I said, sliding it off and handing it back to the salesperson. Without waiting for her to put it back, I turned and started walking toward another case. I let myself look through multiple cases with hundreds of rings before something caught my eye, to my right. I leaned over the counter and looked down at the ring. I immediately knew it was the one. The band consisted of white gold or silver with little diamonds all around it, and at the center was a huge pale blue circle diamond; it was surrounded by more little diamonds in a square. The more I looked at it, the more I loved it. I loved that it wasn't a normal white diamond but blue, my favorite color.

"Can I see this one?" I asked, turning around and seeing both the lady and Liam standing in the same spot. Karen looked at Liam, and he nodded before walking toward me. As I waited for her to come and unlock the case, I looked back down at the ring. It was simple and unique, perfect for me.

"This one is an aquamarine, circle, seven-karat white gold ring." She handed it to me, and I gently took it. I slowly slid it on my ring finger and grinned. It fit me perfectly. Staring down at my hand, I knew I wanted it. The diamond was huge, but if it were smaller, you wouldn't see the blue so well. I almost felt like I would break it as I ran my fingertip across it. It felt weird wearing and seeing a ring on that finger.

"I love it," I breathed.

"It only costs about ten thousand dollars," Karen said as my eyes widened. *What? No, that's way too much.* Sighing inwardly, I slid it off and started handing it over. Guess I'd have to keep looking for one less expensive. Just before the lady could take it from me, Liam's big hand stopped mine.

"We will take it." I turned to him to argue, saying it was too much, but Karen interrupted me.

"But, sir, that isn't one of our finest rings. There are plenty of other ones you—"

"I said we will get it. If my fiancé wants it, then she can get it," he said, his voice hard. Karen swallowed and nodded quickly.

"Yes, sir. Let me go get the paperwork and clean it up. Then you can go." She quickly walked off, giving me time to turn to Liam.

"Liam! That is too much money for a ring," I hissed at him.

"No, it is not."

"Yes, it is. I'll pick another one that's less expensive," I argued.

"Do you have to argue about everything, Jenna? I said we are getting it." He looked down at me, his blue eyes dark and hard. I opened my mouth to reply, but Karen's voice interrupted me. *Wow, that was fast.*

"Mr. Stanford, I just need you to sign here and here." She pointed out a couple of places. Liam did as she asked before handing her a credit card, which she took and left again. I wanted to argue with him about the ring, but I knew I wouldn't win, and a small part of me was excited to actually get an engagement ring that pretty. This would probably be my only wedding, so I might as well enjoy it.

We stood next to each other, not saying a word until Karen came back with stuff in her hands.

"Here you are, sir." She handed him back his credit card. "Also here is the receipt for the ring as well as the box it comes in. I figured your fiancé would like to wear the ring now. We have a lifetime guarantee on any wedding rings, so if the band becomes loose, tight, or even rusts a little, which is normal, just come in and we will fix it for free." Instead of handing me the ring, she handed it to Liam. "Thank you for your business, Mr. Stanford." She shot him a wide smile.

"Thank you, Karen." Liam turned to face me, locking eyes with me. His hand reached for mine and grabbed it, pulling it toward him. I stared into his blue eyes, almost transfixed as his fingers gently caressed mine. I felt warmth on my finger and quickly looked down, away from Liam's gaze, to watch him slide the ring onto my ring finger. I looked from it up to Liam as he raised my hand to his mouth before placing a kiss on my knuckles. I felt my cheeks heat up and felt Karen and a few other people's eyes on us.

The feeling of his soft, smooth lips against my knuckles made a shiver run down my spine. His blue eyes stared intently into mine as his lips lingered longer than necessary. As soon as he pulled away, I felt my knees weaken. It wasn't even a real kiss, but it still had the power to make my legs feel like Jell-o. That made me wonder what would happen when we actually kissed.

With a final nod at Karen, Liam pocketed the receipt as well as the ring box before grabbing my ring-clad hand and leading me out the door. Without speaking, he helped me into the car before coming around and sliding in the driver's seat. I looked down at my left hand and gazed at it in wonder. It felt weird. It was kind of heavy, and when I turned my hand, the blue diamond sparkled. *It's so beautiful.*

"Thank you," I said softly to Liam. I didn't expect a reply, and I didn't get one.

We drove in silence, and I couldn't help but think this was all a dream. Never in my wildest dreams did I think I would ever get a ring at Tiffany and Co., let alone even get married. I had always figured I would die alone or be one of those crazy cat ladies but with dogs instead. The feeling of the car slowing down made me realize we were pulling into the garage.

"So…" I said a moment before Liam turned the car off. "We need to get our story straight."

"We met at a coffee shop by work. Talked, went on a few dates, then fell in love," came his quick response before he got out of the car.

"Liam, that isn't believable," I said, hurrying out of the car after him. His long legs made his stride longer, so every step of his was two for me. He didn't answer me and kept walking down the hall toward the kitchen.

"Liam Stanford, you are going to stop and listen to me right now!" I yelled at him, stopping exactly where I was, putting my hands on my hips. Someone had to be the one to take this seriously, and apparently it was going to be me.

"What did you just say?" His voice was low as he stopped and turned around. I should have felt scared at his expression, but I wasn't.

"You heard me. We need to come up with a believable story that your parents and your sister will believe. The moment we tell them yours, they will know this isn't real. So quit being an ass and help me with a story," I said, my voicing coming out just as low and threatening as his. "And don't look at me like that," I snapped. "If you really want this to work so you can get the business, then you need to start taking this seriously."

I walked past him toward the kitchen to grab a drink and maybe some food. After a minute, I heard him following me. I didn't care if I pissed him off.

He'd pissed me off too many times already, and I would not sit by being the only one serious about this. This was what he wanted me to do and I would do it, but not by myself. Grabbing a glass, I filled it with water before taking a seat at the bar.

I watched Liam open the fridge angrily and take out a container of food. He stomped around the kitchen like a five year old who was told they couldn't have candy. He didn't even glance in my direction as he dished out his food.

"Do you even cook?" I asked out of the blue. I hadn't really had time to go grocery shopping yet, but I would later this week. "Microwaving food gets old." He still didn't reply, and I rolled my eyes. *What a baby.* Liam grabbed his bowl after the microwave beeped, heading to the small kitchen table by the door, which was as far away from me as he could get. It irked me, the way he was acting. Getting up, I went and sat across from him, smiling at his glaring eyes.

"Where should we say we met?" I looked at him, but he just silently ate his food. "I like that idea about the coffee shop. We could say I worked there and we ran into each other one day. How does that sound?" I stared at him, waiting for him to answer. "Liam, I swear to God if you don't say something, I will come over there and cut your balls off. Then I'll tell your parents what is really going on," I threatened him. "You are acting like a child."

"That story sounds fine to me. You saw me and then asked me out that day."

"Liam." I groaned. "You're not helping!"

"You said answer, and I did," he replied. I let my

100

head fall down onto the table, and a bang echoed through the room. Ignoring the pain from my forehead, I sighed deeply.

"You know what? You're no help. We'll just wing it tomorrow, apparently. But one thing we do know is we met at the coffee shop across from your work...what is it called?"

"Juice N Java," he said then stood up, taking his plate to the sink. "Okay, fine. That is our plan." I lifted my head off the table and stood up. My stomach rumbled, and I finally noticed the time. It was a little after seven, and I hadn't eaten since noon, when Lennon let me eat at the mall. I went to the fridge and pulled out a random container of food. The kitchen was silent, and I figured Liam had left. Putting my plate in the microwave, I turned and almost jumped seeing Liam standing there staring at me.

"W-What?" I stuttered.

"Thank you," Liam said, his voice gruff. Without saying anything else, he walked away.

Okayyy.

As I stood there waiting for my food, I looked down at my hand. I didn't know when I would get used to seeing the ring there. Once my food was done, I grabbed a fork and headed to my bedroom to eat. The sun was starting to set, making the hallway glow a light pink and orange. Everything was silent as I made my way to my room and shut the door. When I went to my bed, I stopped, noticing a small red velvet ring box. Remembering Liam had it and that he was kind enough to put it on my bed, a small smile appeared on my face.

I ate in a matter of minutes before sitting there staring at the TV in my room. I'd honestly forgotten about having one in here until now. Deciding to turn in early, I went and changed into my PJs, washed my face, and slipped my ring into its case. Grabbing my dishes, I padded barefoot to the kitchen. After I put them in the dishwasher, I was heading back to my room when I heard a groan. Wondering what it was, I headed down the opposite hall and up the stairs toward a light coming from a room.

When I came to the room, I peeked my head around the corner and saw Liam sitting at his desk, his head in his hands, pulling his brown hair. I wanted to go in and see what was wrong, but knowing I would only get yelled at made me stay where I was. I wished Liam would just cooperate with me and try to be nice. It wouldn't hurt him to do so. Knowing there wasn't anything I could do, I turned and quietly made my way back downstairs before I got caught.

Closing my bedroom door, I leaned against it, wondering about tomorrow. It was going to be very interesting, to say the least. I guess I'd better get my acting on, because if not, this whole deal would be for nothing.

Chapter Nine

I woke up the next morning to a pair of hands shaking me and a voice calling my name. Groaning, I swatted away the hands while mumbling. I think everyone would agree that being woken up by someone is just as bad as an alarm.

"Jenna, get up!" the voice said again right above my head. I rolled over, away from the hands, onto my side. I just wanted to sleep! "Fine, you asked for it." I heard the person's footsteps disappear, and I sighed, snuggling deeper into my pillow.

Just as I got comfortable again, I suddenly felt something wet and cold land on my exposed neck and shoulders. *What is that?* Before I could understand what it was, I was doused in cold water. There wasn't a lot, but there was enough to make my head and my PJ shirt wet. I sat up with a gasp, feeling as the cold water ran down my neck. I turned and stared at a smug Lennon standing next to my bed with an empty cup. I narrowed my eyes at her.

"You know I would have gotten up without the

103

cold water."

"I know." With that, she set the glass on my bedside table. "Okay, up and at 'em. We have a lot to do before you leave."

"But, Lennon, it's nine in the morning!" I whined, looking at the clock. The last few days of being able to sleep in had already got me hooked.

"You have an early lunch and entire day with Liam's parents, so it's time to get up and get ready, or do you want me to get Liam in here?" With one last glare at Lennon, I got up and headed to the shower.

As I showered, I thought about how weird it is to spend the *entire* day with Liam's parents. I thought we were just going to dinner with them, not lunch and dinner. Was that even normal? On that subject, nothing about this was normal. I got out of the warm shower ten minutes later, wrapping a towel around me just in time for Lennon to come barging in.

"Lennon!" I shouted, clenching the towel tighter around me. "Get out!"

"Jenna, come on. It's not like I haven't seen anything like that before." She rolled her eyes at me. I just stood there staring at her like she was crazy. "Okay, fine, I'll leave. Yell for me when you have your underwear and bra on. I'll be right outside your bedroom door." I watched her as she left, waiting to hear my bedroom door close before I even moved a muscle.

Shaking my head, I quickly dried myself off before sliding on my panties and bra. I grabbed a new towel, wrapped the dry one around my body, and wrapped my other one around my head to dry my hair.

"Lennon, you can come in now," I called out, taking a seat at the edge of my bed. She instantly came in, shutting the door behind her.

"Okay, let's get you all dolled up," she said, rubbing her hands together and walking toward me. The look on her face made me not want to go anymore. "Makeup first, clothes second, then your hair," she muttered under her breath as she grabbed my wrist and dragged me to the vanity on the other side of the room. Pushing me down on the seat, she got to work pulling out the drawers that held the makeup we bought yesterday.

"How did those get in there?" I asked, confused. I didn't remember putting those things in there last night.

"I did it while you were in the shower." She waved me off. "Okay, you have great skin, so I'm going to do your makeup light and natural. You don't want your makeup overdone." She talked to herself as she grabbed this and that. I watched her, confused. I didn't really know much about makeup since I had no one to teach me. The only things I knew were mascara because that's a given, foundation to cover up my eye bags, and lipstick. Lennon made me close my eyes so I wouldn't look while she worked.

"What are Liam's parents like?" I asked, breaking the silence.

"They are honestly the nicest people I've ever met. Lily and Adam are like my second parents, and Julie is the sister I always wanted. Being an only child and my parents always gone, I spent more time with Liam and his family than with my own." I sat there silent as she talked. "They'll like you, don't worry." I debated asking her what Liam was like when he was younger, the pictures I'd found of him at the back of my mind. I wanted to know a little bit about him before meeting his parents.

"Lennon...what was Liam like when he was younger?"

"He was the greatest guy ever, and I'm not being biased because I'm his friend. Everyone in school loved him, even the boys. He became the youngest captain for the football team his sophomore year, and they became state champions too. He was on the basketball team, and baseball too. For our school, he was the 'it' kid. He was captain for all three sports and won state two times for football, once for basketball, and twice for baseball." As she spoke about Liam, I stopped myself from saying anything about the rings and pictures I'd seen the other day. "He was basically everybody's favorite person."

"What changed?" I asked before thinking. "Sorry, I didn't mean it like that," I quickly added.

"It's fine. I know what you mean. He isn't the same guy he used to be. He's more shut-off and cold, but once you get past his hard exterior, he can be the most loving, fun, caring guy." I tried not to scoff at that because that sounded nothing like the Liam I knew. I realized that she didn't answer my question, but I didn't push it. It wasn't my place to go asking.

"Do you know why he wants his dad's business

so bad?"

"This business has been his entire life since college. Mr. Stanford always wanted Liam to take over his seat when he was ready, but these last few years all Liam has done is party, chase and sleep with girls, and come into work late, if at all. I can kind of see why he is doing this to Liam. He does need to stop chasing skirts. I know he's only twenty-four and that is the time to live and blah blah blah, but if he wants that seat, he needs to settle down a little." I nodded along with her, thinking about Liam.

"Okay, I am done here. Let's get you dressed. If we don't hurry then Liam will come in here pissed." I followed after her, wanting to make sure she doesn't pick out anything to fancy.

"What are we doing with his parents?" I asked after her.

"I think you guys are just going to their house to eat and get to know one another."

"If we are just going to eat and get to know one another, then why couldn't I sleep in a bit longer?" I questioned, leaning against the wall to my closet.

"Because you are going to their country home, and it's about an hour or two from here. Okay, I found the perfect outfit for you." She turned and held out a pair of dark skinny jeans and a strapless tank top thing. I honestly had no idea what it was called. It was brown with light pink flowers on it. Not arguing with her, I grabbed them and headed back to the bathroom to change.

I did the skinny jean dance, you know where you jump up and down, wiggling into the jeans. I slid on the top, making sure my boobs wouldn't pop out suddenly. After changing, I headed back to my closet.

"That looks great! Now, to finish it off." She handed me a cute brown light sweater to go over top of the shirt and a pair of really cute brown-heeled boots. Putting on some socks and the shoes, I grinned over at Lennon. She definitely knew what she was doing.

"I love this outfit. Thank you."

"No problem. Now let's hurry and do your hair. You need to leave soon." With that, she led me back to the vanity and started on my hair. I closed my eyes automatically. There was no better feeling than someone playing with your hair, and ladies, you will agree with me. In no time, Lennon said she was finished and let me finally open my eyes. I stared at my refection, not really knowing what to say.

I looked like a different person. My long blonde hair was curled into waves down my back, with a few pieces pulled away from my face with bobby pins. My green eyes stood out against dark eye shadow and mascara. My makeup wasn't too bold but instead natural, with light pink blush on my cheeks and light pink lipstick. I stood up and looked at my outfit fully. I looked really cute.

"Thank you, Lenn," I said, turning and grinning at her.

"You're welcome. Here you go." She handed me my bag. "I already put extra lipstick in it, along with everything else you already had in it." I gladly took it before looking around, feeling like I was missing something. *My ring!* Heading to my bedside table, I grabbed my phone and slid it into my pocket before grabbing my ring box. I carefully opened it and smiled softly at my ring. I took it out and slid it onto my index finger. "Is that your ring?" Lennon screeched. I jumped and put a hand over my ear. *And now I'm deaf.*

"Yeah, it is." Before I even finished my sentence, she grabbed my hand and yanked it toward her.

"It is...beautiful!" she exclaimed, staring down at my hand. "Where did you get it?"

"Tiffany's. "

"What! You're so lucky!" Her grip on my wrist tightened, and I tried pulling it away from her.

"Are you girls done yet? We need to leave," I heard Liam say from behind the door. I turned and felt my mouth dry up. He was dressed in a pair of low-ride jeans that looked great on him and a dark blue t-shirt that I knew would make his blue eyes pop even more. His brown hair was slicked back but still slightly messy.

"Yup, she's all good to go," Lennon said, letting my hand go so it flopped to my side. "Have fun and be good, you two." As I walked toward Liam nervously, I felt a hand slap my ass. Turning, I shot Lennon a glare, but she just grinned at me. *She's so weird.*

Silently, we walked to the garage, and I had to force myself not to check out Liam's butt in his jeans. I worried my bottom lip between my teeth as I got into the passenger's seat of the Audi. I'd realized this car was Liam's favorite. Why have all these expensive cars if you only drove one? It was awkward as we sat there silently, Liam driving away from the house.

I turned on the radio, wanting something on instead of silence. Sam Smith's "Lay Me Down" played softly throughout the car and I leaned back in the seat, looking out the window as we passed houses and stores. The chorus of the song started, but before it could continue, the radio was switched off. I turned and glared at Liam, who'd turned it down. Reaching over, I switched it back on and looked back out the window. The same thing happened again, making me snap my gaze over to Liam's. Stubbornly, I turned it back on and glared at the side of Liam's head, almost daring him to do it again. Just as his hand went for the radio, I slapped it.

"No, we are listening to music," I stated. He took his eyes off the road for a second to stare at me.

"Did you just slap my hand away?"

"Yes. Now stop." With that, I turned back to the window. I knew I was being grumpy with him, but I couldn't help it. I was nervous about meeting his family. Would they like me? Sometimes my first impression wasn't all that good. I fidgeted in my seat, going between playing with my hands to biting my lip.

"Are you going to do that the entire drive?" Liam asked, looking at me from the corner of his eye. I immediately stopped playing with my fingers.

"No." But as soon as I said it, my leg started bouncing up and down. "Sorry, I'm just nervous," I admitted after I earned another look from him. He didn't say anything. "You know, for once could you just drop the cold act and actually try to be nice? It's not that hard."

"God, I should have picked someone else," I heard him mutter under his breath.

"What was that? Should have picked someone else? Yes, Liam, you should have picked someone dumber because they wouldn't put up such a fight," I bit out at him.

"You are so annoying! Can't you just shut up and be quiet for once, instead of whining and complaining all the time?" he yelled over at me. Biting my tongue so I wouldn't say anything I would regret later, I turned and glared out the window.

For the next hour, both of us were quiet as we ignored each other. The radio played in the background, but it did nothing to even out the tension. Inside I was fuming at Liam, but it soon faded away as nerves spread through my body the closer we got to Liam's parents' house. The dashboard read noon, showing we had been driving for about an hour and a half. I'd never met anyone's parents before, and I was worried, really worried. The car started to slow down, and Liam turned us off the road onto a driveway. *Oh, God, I'm going to throw up.*

"It's going to be okay," I heard Liam's voice say suddenly. He placed a hand on my thigh, and I jerked my gaze to him. His blue eyes were staring down at me almost kindly. I nodded shakily. "Really, Jenna, it's going to be fine. Just be yourself." *Yeah, like that has worked before. My winning personality has sure helped me out in the past.* His hand squeezed my thigh gently, and I shot him a small smile. The car came to a stop a minute later, in front of a huge home. I stared up at it through the window, already feeling intimidated.

I was so busy staring at the gorgeous brick house that I didn't hear or notice Liam getting out of the car until my door opened. Blushing, I took off my seatbelt and stepped out. Liam reached a hand out to me, and I gladly took it. I was still kind of mad at him, but I needed the support. My hand trembled inside his warm one as he gently tugged me forward. It was weird how normal it felt to hold hands with him and how perfect my hand fit into his.

The closer we got to the door, the more I noticed how big the house actually was. The front yard was big with two tall trees shading the lawn, and from here I could see a cobblestone path that probably led to the backyard. The house was easily on two to three acres of land; it kind of reminded me of a ranch. My foot was about to land on the first step leading to the front door when the deep cherry-red door flew open.

"Liam, my baby!" a female voice yelled from in front of us. Liam dropped my hand to catch the woman who flew at him. I watched as a smile spread across his face. He wrapped his arms around the woman, who I assumed was his mother. As she pulled away from him, I took that moment to study her. She had dark brown hair that went to her shoulders. I couldn't tell what color her eyes were, but I would bet they were the same color as Liam's. She looked to be in her early fifties, if that. Her face wasn't marred by plastic surgery. Instead, I could see the slight wrinkles by her eyes and mouth, indicating she smiled a lot. She stood a little taller than me and was wearing a pretty sundress that showed off her tan arms. After she was done hugging Liam, she turned to me, and I was correct. She had blue eyes just like Liam's, but softer.

"You must be Jenna! I'm Lilly." She smiled at me before engulfing me in a big hug. I was surprised, standing stiff in her arms, but I found myself relaxing instantly and hugging her back. "My, aren't you a pretty little thing?" she said, pulling away but keeping her hands on my shoulders. I blushed from her comment, looking down so my blonde hair would cover my face.

"Is that who I think I it is?" said a deep voice through the door. Lilly moved to my side, swinging an arm around my shoulder. A tall, older, handsome-looking man walked through the door with a wide grin. He stood about six foot two, had brown hair with a little grey in it, and a face like Liam's. Liam had the same cheekbones and jaw line as his father. As Liam's father hugged him, I couldn't help but think he was very handsome for being in his fifties. After hugging Liam, he turned to me, and I was surprised as a pair of grey eyes stared at me. His face was sprinkled with laugh wrinkles, and a few were probably from stress in having to run a company. He smiled kindly at me before coming to a stop just ahead of me. "You must be the girl that has gotten my son tied down." I nodded, not trusting myself to speak.

He suddenly pulled me in for a bone-crushing

hug. I stood still in his arms. This was the third time someone has hugged me in years. For having never met them before, it felt good to be in their arms. They both radiated love and "parent," if that was a thing. Being hugged by a parent figure was different than being hugged by someone else; you felt warm, safe, and protected from everything.

"I'm Adam," he said finally, pulling away from me. "You sure are pretty. What are you doing with a boy like my son?" he joked, grinning widely at me, then at Liam. I looked over at him just in time to see him roll his eyes at his dad but smiling anyways. It was weird seeing Liam relaxed and with a smile. Whenever he's around me he was just cold, his face like a stone.

"Julie's not here yet, but let's head inside and start getting the table ready for lunch." Lilly suggested, nodding at both of us before walking ahead of me into the house. I followed after everyone, and as soon as I passed the entryway, I tried not to gawk at everything or drool from the amazing smell running through the house. The inside was decorated wonderfully with pictures on the walls of most of the family, and what looked like fake flowers were placed in the hallway and probably throughout the house as well.

Following Liam, we went under an archway and came into a pretty kitchen. It was a little bigger than Liam's, with light brown wood and a little dark mixed in with the cabinets, speckled granite counter tops, and a flat stove-top. There was a swinging door on the left side of the kitchen a little further down, which I assumed went to the dining room.

Pots and dishes littered the stove and counter, making the smell of yummy food even stronger than ever.

"Boys, can you grab those plates and bring them to the dining room?" Lilly asked, to which Liam and his father nodded, each grabbing a plate filled with something I didn't get a chance to see. Turning, I saw Lilly struggling to grab enough wine glasses. I quickly ran over to her.

"Here, let me grab those," I said, taking most of them and strategically placing them in my hands and arms so they wouldn't fall. Tell-tale sign I use to be a waitress.

"Oh thank you, hon. Are you okay carrying all of those while I grab the wine?"

"Yeah, I got it." Seeing her move around the kitchen, I instantly knew she did a lot of cooking. She walked around like she owned the room and could probably grab something blindfolded. After she grabbed a bottle of red wine from the fridge, I followed after her to the dining room. I didn't really have the heart to tell her I didn't drink, nor was I of age to do so. Liam's mom set the wine down and started grabbing the glasses from me. I looked around and saw expensive-looking plates and even silverware on the table. I felt like I was in the wrong house. I was used to eating off paper plates or cheap plastic ones from the dollar store, not ones that were easily the amount of my rent.

"I hope you like lasagna, Jenna. I didn't have time to make anything more than that. And I hope you're not a vegetarian," Lilly apologized, looking at me pouring wine into every glass.

"No, that sounds wonderful, and I'm not," I said sincerely. It had been such a long time since I'd had a real homemade meal, that anything sounded good.

"Mom! Dad! Is Liam here yet?" a sudden voice yelled as I heard the front door close, the sound of heels clicking on the tile coming in the kitchen. Before anyone could reply, a gorgeous, tall brunette came into view. She had long, thick dark hair that fell in waves down her back. She was wearing a pair of light blue skinny jeans that showcased her long legs and a cute lace shirt that hugged her upper body. Staring at her, I felt really self-conscious. She had a gorgeous face and just as gorgeous of a body. I felt little and ugly next to her. Liam's parents moved away from the table and hugged her before a pair of matching grey eyes like Adam turned to me. They landed on Liam, who was next to me, her smile widening.

"Baby brother!" She grinned, coming toward us.

"I'm not your baby brother. I'm older than you, dimwit," Liam said but grinned widely at his sister, coming around the dining table to hug her.

"Well, you act like a baby even though I am the youngest, so that makes me older than you," she retorted. I held back my grin, liking the way she talked to Liam. "And you are Jenna," she said, once her and Liam had separated. It seemed like everyone already knew me.

"And you must be Julie," I said, rubbing my sweaty palms on my jeans and sending her a small smile. I was surprised yet again as she pulled me into a hug.

"I am. It's nice to meet the girl who tamed my

116

brother," she said, pulling away. We were all silent for a minute, and I quickly took that time to look her over. Liam or even Lennon hadn't told me what Julie did for a living, and I couldn't ask her point blank since I'm supposed to already know. Just from first glance I figured she was a model. With her tall, slim body and good looks, she had to be one. In the second I'd seen her walk in, that confirmed my theory. Having worked at the diner for hours with nothing to do, I would people watch, and I got pretty good at it. It was actually pretty sad that I could figure out a random stranger's life but not my own. I turned to Lilly after Julie and studied her. Liam's father, of course, founded their company, but from looking at Lilly I could tell she wasn't really a business type of person. She seemed more free, or at the very least less uptight. Seeing as the house was beautifully decorated, I was also going to guess she was a designer. I really hoped my guesses were right or I'd make an utter fool out of myself.

"Okay, let's eat," Lilly said, clapping her hands. We all moved to the table at the same time. Going around to the opposite side of Lilly and Adam, Liam pulled out my chair for me. I shot him a smile in thanks, taking a seat. He sat to my left, Julie sat at the end of the table to my right, and Liam's parents sat across from us. I grabbed the napkin under my silverware and placed it in my lap, watching as Lilly stood up and spooned portions of lasagna onto everyone's plate. Liam grabbed mine and held it out for his mom before placing it back in front of me.

"There is plenty more, you guys, after you're done. I made extra, just in case." Once everyone had their plates filled with food, Adam raised his wine glass.

"To Jenna. I know we have just met you, but I can already tell you are perfect for my son," he said with a smile at me. "You're already great for putting up with him. Cheers." I laughed softly and clinked glasses with everyone. I took a small sip and had to force myself not to make a face. To me it tasted bitter, but I didn't want to offend anyone.

"Nice, Dad," Liam said, shaking his head and taking a bite of his garlic bread. When I took a bite of my lasagna, I almost moaned. It tasted amazing!

"So, Jenna, tell us a little bit about yourself. Liam here hasn't been too forthcoming about you." Feeling all nervous again, I swallowed my food.

"There's not really much to tell," I said quietly.

"Yes there is. About how old are you?" Lilly prompted, eating her food and looking at me patiently, waiting for an answer. I felt Liam's father and sister staring at me as well, waiting.

"I am nineteen. I'll be twenty in a few weeks." She raised an eyebrow at my age but didn't say anything, thankfully. "I, uh, grew up here in New York, and I work at a coffee shop called Juice N' Java," I said, not wanting to talk about myself.

"Isn't that the place across from the office?" Lilly asked, turning to Liam.

"Yes, it is. That is how Jenna and I actually met," Liam answered, reaching for his wine. She nodded at him.

"How are your parents taking this engagement,

Jenna? Are they excited? I bet they and your siblings were surprised," Adam said suddenly. I instantly froze at the mention of my parents. This was the part I had been dreading. I was hoping the subject wouldn't come up, but I knew that thought would be too good to be true. I didn't want to say anything and get their pity. They all sat there waiting in silence for my answer, even Liam. I could tell Liam was confused on why I wasn't answering, but my throat seemed to be clogged. Feeling all of their gazes, I forcefully swallowed, knowing I had to answer.

"I...I don't have any parents or siblings," I said softly, looking down at my plate.

"Oh...I..." Adam trailed off, obviously looking over at Lilly for help.

"We're so sorry, Jenna," Lilly said, her voice filled with sincerity and sadness. I looked up at them, sending them all a small smile.

"It's okay. It was a long time ago." I could tell they knew I didn't want to talk about it anymore, so Julie started talking. I could have hugged her in that moment.

"How long ago did you guys meet?" she asked, chewing and waiting for our answer.

"About a year ago," I answered before I could stop myself. I felt Liam's hand suddenly on my thigh, squeezing it, making me look toward him.

"That's weird. I thought you were still with Carmen a year ago," Julie pointed out, clearly confused.

"Well, we met a year ago, but we didn't start dating for a while. It was a good two months before we even went on our first date. I had spilt coffee all over his suit the first day we met," I lied. Time to get my acting on. "He wasn't the happiest at that moment, and he didn't say anything to me. He just walked out." I turned and faked a smile up at Liam. He seemed surprised at first but quickly recovered.

"Sounds like Liam," she said, grinning and shaking her head.

Thankfully no one asked anymore questions after that, but I knew after dinner Liam and I were going to have to come up with some good lies to tell his family. I sat there, quietly eating and watching as everyone talked to each other. Liam seemed relaxed and had a carefree look on his face, which made me wonder why he acted so cold toward me. Lilly and Adam included me in their conversations, and I could feel myself relaxing and enjoying myself throughout the meal. Something about Liam's family pulled at something inside of me that I hadn't felt before. I felt myself letting down my walls a little bit as I smiled and laughed.

Chapter Ten

Lunch and dinner went by smoothly after the awkward conversation about my parents. Thankfully, Liam's parents didn't say anything else about it, and I was actually starting to relax around them. They were definitely different than I'd originally assumed; I thought they would stuck-up and rude, but instead they were all really nice and pretty sarcastic when they wanted to be. Lilly, Liam's mom, was very down to earth and was always smiling. Adam, Liam's father, was just as nice and seemed to always have something to say, even if it was just a sarcastic remark. And Julie, Liam's sister, was mix of both her parents; she was really sarcastic and witty and made everything less tense. I knew I would be getting along with her just fine.

We had just finished eating and were sitting there when Julie suddenly gasped and looked at me with wide eyes. I looked at her confused and then looked up at Liam next to me.

"Is that your ring?" The moment Julie said it,

Lilly snapped her head toward me. Her blue eyes looked down at my hands, which were on the counter. I had actually forgotten it was there.

"It is…beautiful!" Lilly exclaimed, grinning widely at Liam and me. "You have to tell us how Liam proposed to you, Jenna!"

"Yes. Was it sweet and amazing?" Julie joined in.

"Liam, you tell it the best," I said, turning to him and smiling sweetly at him. He glared down at me.

"No, you do, sweetie," he bit out. I shot him a look, but an idea popped in my head. *Well, he asked for it.*

"Okay. Well, we had already been going out for eight months when Liam all of a sudden started acting weird and rude. He kept pushing me away and wouldn't answer my calls or texts," I said.

"Liam!" His mother turned and glared at him. I stifled my laughter at the glares Lilly and Julie sent Liam, who in turned glared at me.

"After about three days of avoiding me, he suddenly showed up at my work and asked me to go on a date. Since I was really in love with him, I said yes, although I was hurt. Anyways, that night he picked me up and drove toward the beach. For our second date, he took me to the beach after a romantic dinner. As we pulled up and walked a little ways in the sand, we came to a stop in front of a blanket and candles. Apparently Liam here had someone set it up for us while we were on our way." I plastered a smile on my face, looking at Liam and moving my hand up his arm. "He was so nervous and kept stuttering as we sat there. After a while of him trying to say something, he finally got down on his knee just as the sun was setting. It was perfect, aside from his nervousness and his red face." My hand was now on his shoulder, squeezing it. "He acted the way he did because he was scared of my answer and wanted it to be a surprise."

"Awww, that is so sweet," Lilly cooed, smiling at us.

"Honey." Liam looked down at me. "I don't remember it being that way."

"It was, sweetie pie, but it was perfect." I squeezed his upper arm hard, but he didn't even flinch. Any opportunity to embarrass him, I was going to take it.

"Look at you two." I held back my smirk. Hey, if Liam wanted me to tell the story of our proposal, then he'd better like what I'd come up with. "Let me go get the dessert really quick," Lilly said suddenly, standing up.

"Here, let me help you," I offered, feeling Liam's hand tighten down on my thigh.

"No, you're the guest, you sit down. Adam, you can come help me?" She shot Liam's father a look, silently telling him to get up.

They left the room, and I sat there awkwardly, feeling the warmth of Liam's hand on my thigh soaking through my jeans.

"You're going to pay for that later," Liam suddenly whispered in my ear. His warm breath tickled my neck, and his voice was deep, making a shiver run down my spine.

"So, Julie, you're a model?" I asked, breaking the silence and Liam's hold on me.

123

"I am, actually." She grinned over at me. Relief ran through me. I was right and didn't make a fool of myself. "Right now I'm one of the Victoria's Secret models."

"Wow, that's amazing. I thought I recognized you from somewhere." When I was sitting in my room bored watching TV the other day, several commercials came up for Victoria's Secret, and Julie had been one of the girls. "How did you get into modeling?"

"I honestly don't know. I kind of just went with it a few years ago, and now I love it. I don't always do Victoria's Secret campaigns. Sometimes I do other modeling, but it's mostly on the side. Right now I'm doing both modeling and going to school."

"Oh, wow. What university are you going to?"

"Columbia. How about you? Are you attending a university?" Julie asked, drinking her wine and looking at me.

"Um, no, not at the moment." I'd never really thought about going to college. I'd just been so focused on trying to make ends meet that college wasn't even in the picture. I'd graduated high school, but barely. I was more absent than not because I had to watch some of the younger kids at the home while everyone was at work. Sitting next to everyone who had or was going to college made me feel very stupid.

"That's okay. College isn't for everyone," Julie said kindly just as her parents came back into the room. They both carried plates with some kind of pie that looked amazing.

"Here you go. Jenna, I hope you like blueberry

pie," Lilly said, placing a plate in front of me.

"Thank you. It looks great. Did you make it yourself, Mrs. Stanford?"

"Oh please, call me Lilly. I didn't make it. I actually bought it at the store. I can't make a pie this good." She chuckled, taking a seat as everyone dug into their pies. As I took a bite, I held back a moan at how good it was. Who knew blueberry pie could be so delicious?

We ate in silence, and I glanced around at everyone. Liam was strangely quiet the entire meal, only saying a few words. He was eating in complete silence, not even paying attention to anything else. Julie was eating her pie slowly while occasionally looking at Liam and me, and Liam's parents seemed to be in a silent argument, giving each other pointed looks. I ducked my head, not wanting to be caught staring.

"So, Liam and Jenna…" Lilly's voice broke the silence, making all of us look at her. She seemed to be trying to decide if she should say what she wanted to or not. "When is the wedding?" she finally blurted out. She looked a little ashamed, but not really. She sat there, staring at us expectantly.

Not knowing what to say, I turned to Liam, who thankfully was looking at me too. I asked him what we should do with my eyes, and he seemed to get the hint.

"We haven't decided just yet," came his simple, yet perfect, response.

"You haven't thought about the date, location, guests, anything?" Lilly looked like she was about to have a heart attack any moment.

"No, Mother, we haven't. We've only been engaged a few weeks."

"It's okay, no need to stress. I'll help you guys get everything ready, and so will Julie. We are going to make this the greatest wedding ever," Lilly said, taking deep breaths. "We have so much to do!" She clapped her hands together. I stared at her wide-eyed, not really liking the excited look she had on her face. Why did I have a feeling this wedding was going to be over the top?

"We need to get a date set, then think about a theme, guests, and bridesmaids! And a dress!" Lilly rambled, not even stopping to take a breath of air.

"Honey, not right now. We can figure that out later," Adam said, putting his hand on his wife's arm.

"Sorry, you are right. I'm just so excited." Her blue eyes sparkled.

"How about we take this to the living room?" Adam asked, sliding his chair back. Everyone got up and out of their seats. As Adam, Liam, and Julie started walking out, I looked at the table and saw it was still covered with dirty plates. The room was emptied a second later, and the waitress in me started piling up the plates, balancing them all in my arms. Using my butt, I opened the swinging door to the kitchen and set them by the sink. I knew I was the guest here and should be out there with them, but I needed a moment.

I started washing the dishes, thinking about everything. Liam's parents seemed to buy our lie about how we met and when we got engaged. I always thought that when I got engaged it would be really sweet and real, not some made-up scheme with a guy I didn't even know and who didn't like me. I already felt bad about lying to Liam's parents, especially after how nice they had been to me today. They seemed like really nice people, and I didn't even want to begin thinking about how they'd act when they learned this was all fake. It was honestly very sad that I had stooped this low, lying to strangers for money. I had only a few dishes cleaned when Lilly suddenly appeared out of nowhere, scaring me.

"There you are! What are you doing?" she asked. I jumped and put a wet hand to my chest.

"Lilly, you scared me." I put my hands back in the sink.

"Honey, you don't have to clean those. I can do them later." She tried to stop me, but I shook my head.

"No, it's fine, honestly. I need to help with something. I'd feel better if I did." I felt her staring at me before she moved to my right side, grabbing a towel.

"You wash and rinse, and I'll dry," she said, taking a plate from my hand and drying it. I nodded, a small smile upon my lips. We silently washed and dried for a few minutes. "You know, you are the first girl to ever offer to help," Lilly said suddenly.

"Oh?" I already kind of knew I wasn't the first girl Liam had brought over to meet his parents.

"I mean he has only brought home two girls, but they never even lifted a finger to do anything. Not that I really care since I don't mind doing it, but even the thought would be nice. I think you're perfect for my son," she said and glanced over at me.

"B-but you hardly even know me," I stuttered, surprised by her remark. She just shrugged.

"I don't need to know a lot to know you're the right one. Thank you for helping me clean." She changed the subject before I could say anything.

"It's no problem. I grew up in a home, and all of us always had a chore to do. I was one of the oldest, so I did more than the little kids, but one of mine was doing the dishes."

"I don't mean to pry, but how long were you there?" Lilly asked softly.

"My mom left me when I was five, and I emancipated myself at seventeen." I found myself opening up to her, and I couldn't figure out why. I was usually a closed book, but there was something about Lilly that made me want to tell her stuff; maybe it was her mother vibe. "The home wasn't that bad, honestly. I mean, it had its down times, but my time spent there wasn't horrible. There had been about six of us at the one home; it was me and another guy my age, a boy two years younger than us, and three little ones who were about three to six. Two girls and a little boy." I thought back to the kids and smiled.

Matt, the guy my age, who had been sixteen at the time, was okay. He never really had anything to do with any of us. He mostly kept to himself and stayed in his room. Ryan, the boy two years younger than me, was kind of the same but slightly more outgoing. Sometimes he would play with me and the three little ones, but he would always be a little reserved and kept to himself most of the time. Then you had the three little ones; Carrie was the oldest of the three at the age of six, and she was an angel always helping me. Then there was Thomas, the middle one at four, who was rambunctious and liked to get into everything, and finally Lea, the youngest at three, who was the cutest thing ever.

Of course the girls were my favorite, but even Thomas had a piece of my heart. When the foster caretakers were busy with work, I watched all three, and we kind of became our own group. Right before I had turned seventeen, all three of them had gotten adopted, thankfully. I was grateful and sad that they were going away, but I didn't want them to stay here like I was. They deserved nice, loving families. That was kind of why I emancipated myself a little after I turned seventeen, because I felt even more alone. The two other boys never talked to me after the kids left, so I decided I was ready to leave. After graduating, I packed my stuff and left.

I hadn't realized I was rambling until my hand hit the empty sink and the clink of the glass plate being put away filled my ears.

"I'm sorry. I've just been rambling," I said, apologizing.

"You're fine, Jenna, really. I was the one who asked," Lilly said, putting a hand on my shoulder. I smiled back at her, feeling my stomach churn.

A part of me was happy that I'd told someone about a little bit of my childhood and also glad that Lilly didn't interrupt me or even judge. But the other part of me was upset with myself for easily spilling stuff about my life, and the worst part was that feeling was starting to overcome the other. I could almost physically feel myself closing myself in, like a book shutting its front cover. Shutting out my emotions was something I'd always done. Not being able to feel anything was better than feeling it all and getting hurt. *Don't get close enough to anyone because they are just going to leave and hurt you.* That used to be my mantra, but now that I'd felt a little of what a family was like, I didn't feel like doing that anymore.

I knew getting close to Liam's family would only hurt me and them, but I could already feel myself starting to. Hell, I just told Lily stuff about my life that it took even Sophia months to get out of me. I was walking on dangerous ground already, and we weren't even close to the end of the year. If I wanted to make it out of the deal unscathed, then I needed to stop myself from forming a bond with the family, but could I do that? Could I go back to being shut-off and lonely?

***

Liam

I didn't know about Jenna's parents, and to say I was shocked was an understatement. I wasn't really that shocked at the news but more of why she didn't tell me when I called her a "spoiled rich daddy's girl." I knew I should have known that before I brought her here, but I couldn't let myself become interested in her. I didn't plan on falling for her, and I wouldn't. Getting to know Jenna would somehow make this deal something more than a deal, and I wouldn't let that happen. Hell, I didn't even know she was only nineteen! She looked a lot older than she actually was.

Yes, I felt bad for Jenna not having a family growing up. That would be terrible for any child. If I didn't have such great parents, I honestly didn't know how I would live. I loved my family immensely.

I was sitting there at the table taking in Jenna's news, same as my parents and sister. Next to me, I could practically feel the nerves radiating off of Jenna. I didn't know how to comfort her, so all I did was squeeze her thigh. During rest of lunch and dinner, I spaced out thinking about Jenna. Yes, she was different, very different than the girls I had been with during the last few years. She didn't seem to care about fashion, her looks, or what people thought of her, and I'd started to think that she didn't care about money. That wasn't really true, however, since she did take the deal for the money.

Something about Jenna intrigued me. I felt myself turning my body as she talked to my parents, my hand resting on her thigh the entire meal, and I kept looking at her face. I hadn't spent any time with her and now, sitting here at the table, I'd started to notice she talked a lot using her hands. She could hold her own in a conversation, and she blushed easily. She was definitely different than the other girls; she didn't scream confidence. Instead, she seemed like the type to stand off to the side so others got attention while she observed.

The sound of Julie practically squealing jerked

me out of my thoughts and back to the present. I caught onto the conversation when my mom asked us how I proposed. My mind seemed to blank of a story my mother would believe.

"Liam, you tell it the best," Jenna said, placing her hand on my arm. She was looking at me with those wide green eyes that seemed to sparkle with mischief. I could tell she wanted me to say it so I'd mess up or something.

"No, you do, sweetie," I bit out, not liking the endearment on my tongue.

"Okay. Well..." Jenna started instantly, and I knew I'd fallen for the trap. She wanted me to say that so she could make me look bad. As she continued on with the make-believe story that would never happen in a million years, I narrowed my eyes at her. She was making me sound like a stuttering wimp, and I was anything but that. The more she lied, the more my nice thoughts and feelings flew out the window.

"Awww, that is so sweet," my mom cooed, smiling at us.

"Honey." I looked down at her, clenching my jaw. "I don't remember it being that way." *How was my mother buying into that?*

"It was, sweetie pie, but it was perfect." She squeezed my upper arm hard, but it honestly felt like a small pinch. *Man, she's weak.*

"Awww, look at you two," Mom said, grinning like an idiot at us. Beside me I watched Jenna's lips twitch, like she was holding back a smile. "Let me go get dessert really quick." Mom had really gone all out on this one. Jenna asked if she could help, and I quickly squeezed her thigh, warning her I wanted to talk to her about what just happened. Thankfully, my mom brushed her off and my father got up to help.

"You're going to pay for that later," I whispered into her ear, satisfied by her reaction.

Jenna turned to Julie a few minutes later, asking her about modeling. I tuned them out, not wanting to hear their girl talk. It didn't surprise me that Jenna knew my sister was a model. Lennon must have told her. As I thought of Lennon, I realized I needed to talk to her; I didn't want her to get close to Jenna. I didn't need any more issues or drama concerning this deal. The moment Lennon found out, and I had to tell her since she was going to be Jenna's 'assistant,' she flipped. By the end of her rant, I felt like my ears were going to fall off. I didn't understand why she freaked out the way she did, but whatever.

"So, Liam and Jenna…" my mom said, making me turn my gaze toward her. I instantly knew what she was going to ask. She was never one for letting things slide by. "When is the wedding?" I looked down at Jenna just in time for her to turn to me, her eyes wide.

"We haven't decided just yet," I said, not really knowing what else to say.

"You haven't thought about the date, location, guests, anything?" Mom looked like she was about to have a heart attack any moment.

"No, Mother, we haven't. We've only been engaged a few weeks."

"It's okay, no need to stress. I'll help you guys

get everything ready, and so will Julie. We are going to make this the greatest wedding ever." She fanned her face with her hands. "We have so much to do!" She clapped. "We need to get a date set, then think about a theme, guests, and bridesmaids! And a dress!" I groaned inwardly, knowing my mother would make this wedding over the top. Having your mother be a designer wasn't the greatest sometimes.

"Honey, not right now. We can figure that out later," my father said, putting his hand on my mother's arm.

"Sorry, you're right. I'm just so excited."

I ran a hand down my face, already thinking about how this wedding was going to be a disaster.

The rest of dessert thankfully went by fast. I was more than ready to get Jenna out of here as quickly as possible. Once we got to the living room like my father suggested, I could make up a lie so we could leave. I could already see my mother and sister taking a liking to her, and I didn't know if that was a good idea, especially for my mother. She could get attached pretty easily, and if she got attached to Jenna, at the end of the year she would be heartbroken. It was just better that my family didn't like Jenna too much, so this all could work out. If not, everything would have just gone down the drain.

Chapter Eleven

Jenna

Bored. Lonely. Those two terms I had become very familiar with. It was now Sunday morning, exactly five days since I'd met Liam's parents, and five days of doing absolutely nothing. I hadn't seen Liam since we visited his parents, and it was starting to annoy me. I thought he would be here this weekend and maybe, just maybe, we could "bond," but apparently not.

Right after my talk with his mother, when I walked into the living room, he was out of his seat and ready to leave. I barely had time to say goodbye to his family before Liam was pushing me out the door and into the car. I tried asking why we were leaving so soon when I had just started to bond with them. All I got in reply was, "We are going home" or a grunt. The moment we got home, which was around four, Liam walked away from me down the hall, and that was the last time I had seen him. He was always gone before I got up in the morning and

135

was always getting home after I was already in bed.

I'd heard him moving around late at night but hadn't gotten the guts to get up and go talk to him. I was still confused as to why we had to leave his parents and why he was still acting cold with me. You'd think he'd want to get to know me better or something, but no. He'd made himself scarce lately.

The last five days hadn't been altogether unproductive, though. On Wednesday, I called Candy and talked to her for a few hours. I also went grocery shopping that afternoon with Garrett, who was actually really great company. On Thursday, I met up with Sophia at the diner to get my last paycheck and catch up. We spent a good three hours just sitting there talking before she had to get back to work. Ever since I went shopping, I'd cooked from home. I even made extras for Liam, but he was never there. Although I did notice in the morning the leftovers would be gone, so at least he was eating. On Friday, I had my first encounter with Liam's maid, Martha.

I had just gotten out of the shower and was headed to get a drink in just my towel when I came across Martha in the kitchen. Both of us were surprised, to say the least. Martha at first thought I was one of Liam's lady friends, but I explained to her that I wasn't without going into too much detail. Martha was a small, slight woman in her mid-sixties with short white hair. She looked to be what I thought a grandma would be like. Apparently she was supposed to clean the house twice a week, but she'd been busy with her grandchildren so she couldn't come by.

136

We ended up spending a good portion of the morning talking and getting to know one another. I didn't tell her I was Liam's fake fiancé, and she thankfully didn't ask. I kept my ring in my bedroom, and Martha just thought I was the daughter of some friend of Liam's. I had already told enough people about the deal that I didn't want to get in trouble telling anyone else.

Now, on Sunday morning, I sat outside out in the gazebo looking out at the flowers, enjoying the nice weather. It was so nice out that I was even in shorts, but I knew the nice weather wouldn't last much longer. With nothing else to do, I thought about taking a swim. There wasn't much I hadn't done inside the house. I'd already finished two books in just a few days, and I'd cleaned the house, although it didn't need it. I'd even walked around the backyard multiple times. I guess redecorating would be on my to-do list this week.

Deciding to take advantage of the weather, I headed inside to change into a bathing suit. I didn't remember having one or even buying one, but yesterday, bored, I'd gone through my clothes and found one. Lennon must have snuck it in while we were shopping. I headed into my room and stripped out of my current clothes and grabbed my new swim suit. Putting it on, I couldn't help but love it.

The top was almost tie dye, but with more white. It had a fringe hanging down the front, and the bottom was the same tie-dye pattern. I normally didn't like my body, but as I looked in the mirror, I smiled at myself, turning in different poses. I quickly pulled my blonde hair into a messy bun on top of my head. With a towel hanging off my arm, I headed back outside.

As I walked toward the pool, I couldn't help but think of how bored and lonely I had been this week. Sure, I'd always been lonely, but not ever really bored. Working two jobs every day until late at night didn't give me much time to be bored. And when I had a day off from both, I was too busy catching up on sleep, cleaning my little apartment, or paying bills. Now that I had no jobs, or anything to do for that matter, I was *very* bored. I just wished Liam would give me something to do or let me get another job. I was not good at doing nothing because I would soon start thinking about things I shouldn't, and that was not good. Someone like me had to be going and doing something.

With a sigh, I set my towel on a bench next to the pool and made my way to the stair entrance. When I dipped my toe in, I shivered a little at the coldness. Deciding it would be better to just get in quickly, I went to the end of the deep end and took a deep breath. Before I could back out, I was jumping into the water and letting it envelop me in a cocoon, my body sinking to the bottom. Once I hit the bottom, I pushed off from the floor and swam to the surface. My head broke the surface of the water, and I gulped in air, feeling the cool water against my skin.

I grinned, moving my arms around me to stay afloat. It'd been so long since I swam last that it felt amazing. As a kid, I would walk to the Rec Center whenever I could and swim for a while before heading back home. I loved the feeling of water against my skin and how weightless I felt floating on top of it. Turning to drift on my back, I closed my eyes, feeling my body let go. The feeling of being weightless and free was something I treasured. I didn't have many opportunities to feel that way in my life. Instead, I often felt weighed down, the whole weight of the world resting on my shoulders.

The sun shone bright on me, warming the skin that wasn't underwater, a slightly breeze tickling it. A few birds chirped and sang around me, talking to one another. A sense of calm washed over me, and I grinned widely. Dunking my head back under, I started swimming to the other side.

I swam from one end of the pool to the other multiple times before coming to a stop at the deep end and resting my arms on the edge. I didn't realize how big the pool was until I did a lap. My arms burned. After doing three laps, my arms felt like noodles. Softly kicking my legs, I rested my head on my arms on the corner of the pool and closed my eyes, feeling the soft breeze against my face. Lying there, I realized I could get use to this. A pool at my disposal was going to be nice when summer came around. I debated getting up and turning on some music, but I was being lazy and didn't want to get out.

I lost track of time swimming around in the pool and occasionally getting out to try and get a little bit of a tan. I was now on my back, floating again, when a muffled voice reached my ears underwater. When I opened my eyes, I saw Liam standing there in his work clothes, his hands in his pant pockets.

He must have taken off his suit, since he was only wearing a nice-fitting light grey shirt with the sleeves rolled up and a pair of black slacks, his tie loosened and hanging around his neck. His brown hair was tousled, and he had a nice five o'clock shadow across his jaw. All in all, he looked very sexy standing there, watching me.

Surprised to see him home, I swam toward him and stopped treading water, looking up at him.

"You're home."

"What are you doing in the pool?" he asked with a raised eyebrow.

"Swimming, what else?" I replied sarcastically.

"It's almost six thirty. It's going to be dark soon." *Oh.* It was three when I'd first got in, so I'd been in here for three and a half hours!

"Shit," I muttered under my breath, going to the edge and pulling myself out of the pool. I kicked my legs a little to help me and swung my leg onto the concrete. Liam took a small step back as I stood there, dripping wet. I felt him look down my body, which my bikini did little to cover up. With my cheeks red, I quickly brushed past him and grabbed my towel. The whole time I dried off my arms and legs, I felt Liam's gaze on me, and I tried not to squirm. I bent over to dry my legs and heard a quiet groan. I shot back up and blushed even harder, turning to his direction.

"Are you done yet?" he asked in a deep, husky voice. I could see his hands balled into fists. I quickly wrapped my towel around myself as my stomach growled, ready for dinner.

"Are you hungry?" I asked, walking toward

140

Liam and trying to hide the sounds my stomach was making. All he did was nod, looking down at me, his blue eyes darker than before. Swallowing quickly, I walked past him and toward the house, the whole time feeling his heated stare. Not knowing if he was following me, I swiftly went to my room and threw on an oversized t-shirt. I didn't have time to change because I bet Liam would want dinner done fast.

I came back into the kitchen and found Liam standing there, looking down at his phone. Tearing my eyes away from his sexy form leaning against the counter, I headed to the fridge.

"Do you want something specific?" I asked, looking around.

"No," came his only reply. Rolling my eyes, I decided to make something quick and simple. I grabbed some shrimp from the freezer and quickly put it in a bowl with some water. I pulled out a big pan along with some spaghetti noodles. As I moved around the kitchen, Liam just stood there playing on his phone and occasionally looking over at me. I tried not to let his gaze affect me while I worked.

With the noodles boiling with a little bit of salt for our shrimp linguine, I grabbed what I would need from the fridge for the sauce. With nothing to do while the noodles were cooking, I leaned against the counter by the sink and watched Liam. He leaned against the counter like a model who'd just come off the runway. I ran my eyes greedily down his body, actually feeling my mouth water. There was nothing sexier then a well-dressed man. "I think your noodles are over boiling," Liam said suddenly. I quickly looked away from him and to the stove. He was right. I quickly ran to it and grabbed the spoon, stirring it just before it boiled over the side. Tasting a piece of a noodle and noticing it was done, I turned off the stove and went to grab the food to drain it. "I got it," Liam's deep voice said over my shoulder, his hands coming over mine. As I looked up, Liam stood pressed against me, grabbing the pan's handle. His leg nudged for me to move, so I stepped to my left.

I watched as he picked up the full pan of hot water and dumped it in the drainer. Once all the noodles were out of the pan, he shook the drainer of water before putting the noodles back in the pan. I stared at him, surprised. He put it back on the stove and turned to me. I raised an eyebrow at him.

"You know how to cook?" I asked.

"Of course," he said, looking at me weird.

"Sorry, I thought you had someone cook for you and put it in the fridge in containers," I admitted. I never would have pegged Liam as a guy who could cook.

"I do that because it's easier when I work early or late." I nodded, biting back a smile. I moved around him so I could finish our meal. Liam was finally talking to me, and I wasn't going to say anything to mess it up.

Stirring the noodles and the buttery wine sauce, I asked Liam to bring me the shrimp before dumping them in. As usual, the shrimp cooked in just a minute and then our food was done. While I'd been stirring the pot, Liam had gotten us bowls, and he was waiting for me to plate the food. Once I was done, I put mine on the dining table before grabbing a drink.

We sat there awkwardly, eating quietly, not saying a word to one another. Dinner was good, and I was eating mine not so gracefully, unlike Liam. But hey, when you've been outside for hours swimming, it makes you hungry. The silence continued, and I shifted awkwardly in my seat. I normally didn't mind silence, but Liam just sat there staring at me. Clearing my throat, I opened my mouth, whatever came to mind coming out.

"So you played all different kinds of sports in high school?" I asked, taking a sip of water. The moment I asked, I knew I probably shouldn't have. Liam's face darkened, and his cobalt eyes narrowed. He didn't say anything for a full minute. He just glared at me. "I'm not allowed to ask that?" I asked, narrowing my own eyes at him.

I hated the way he looked at me, and that the moment I said one little thing, he flipped. Was I not allowed to even *try* and get to know him? At least I was trying to make an effort, unlike him. I'd enough of his looks and glares. If he wanted me to pretend like he wasn't there, then so be it.

"No, you are not." His voice was low.

"What is that, taboo or something? Am I not supposed to know you have five championship rings for different sports?"

"It is none of your concern." For some reason, that made me even angrier. There went any happy feelings I had from earlier.

"How is that none of my concern, Liam? I don't know you! How are we supposed to make this work

143

if you won't even try? I do not want to be here, but at least I'm trying to do something, unlike you." I stood up, pushing my chair backwards across the tile. "You know what? Have it your way. If you want to act like I don't exist, then fine. I'll do the same to you. I'm done trying." With that, I left my empty plate on the table and walked off to my room.

Muttering under my breath at how much of an idiot Liam was, I didn't notice or hear him walking after me. All I wanted to do was slap him until he got some common sense and started acting like a real person, not some cold, mean, distant guy. Sure, he was hot, super hot, but his personality was the thing that made him unattractive. Grumbling, I reached for my door, but instead of opening it, I was turned around and pushed against it. With a gasp, I looked up into Liam's eyes. He towered over me, pressing my body against my bedroom door. A voice in the back of my head kept telling me to push him away, but my arms wouldn't work, nor my mouth either, it seemed.

"Why do you think it is your 'right' to know everything about me, Jenna? Why are you so curious about me?" he asked lowly, staring down at me. One of his hands moved to my arm and ran up it, sending shivers all over my body. "You don't seem to take no for an answer, and you seem to love to flap your mouth. Didn't your parents teach you it's wrong to intrude on other peoples' lives?" he hissed. I tried not to let my heart fall at his words, but it did anyways. He knew I didn't have parents, yet he still had to rub it in my face. Seeing my fallen face, his eyes widened. "Jenna—"

"Liam, don't," I whispered.

"I'm sorry. I didn't mean for that to come out. I…You." He shook his head. I watched him as he seemed to have an internal debate. He groaned and lowered his head, resting his forehead on my shoulder, his warm breath blowing along my neck. I stiffened at the connection, surprised Liam was even touching me. "What are you doing to me?" I heard him whisper against my neck. If he wasn't so close to my ear, I wouldn't have heard him. "I'm sorry," he said quietly before pulling away and walking toward his room, disappearing from view.

I stood there, leaning against my door in shock. Two times now, Liam had said sorry to me. I stared at the spot he'd just occupied, my mind racing. What did he mean, what have I done to him? I leaned there, different emotions running through my mind. I knew I should be angry at him for pressing me against a door and yelling at me, but I felt the opposite. My arm tingled from his touch, and my heart was still racing. *No, Liam, what are* you *doing to me?*

Chapter Twelve

The next morning, Monday, I forced myself to get up early so I could get a head start. It took me a while to get up because I'd spent most of the night tossing and turning. I couldn't get Liam out of my head, and it was starting to drive me nuts. The look on his face when he pulled away from me and left still kept repeating in my mind. He looked confused and lost. With all different kinds of emotions swirling inside of me, I pushed them to the side as I got up.

As I walked into the kitchen, I decided I was going to spend the day redecorating. I had no idea what I wanted to do yet, but at the very least I could go around and try to get an idea. Getting a cup of coffee, I headed to the living room first. The place was very nice, but it didn't scream *home*. Nothing about the house did. It just seemed cold and lonely. All I wanted to do was either paint it a new color or add some furniture and pictures.

The clock read 7:45 as I walked around the living room, taking in everything. The room was a

146

color I loved, a deep blue. The only thing I think the room needed was a few bright pictures and/or decorations scattered around. With a nod, I turned and headed back down the hall. I knew I wasn't a designer, but I had some fashion sense.

After looking in my room, the kitchen, and the library, I realized none of them needed much done. Putting my coffee cup away, I remembered there was a room next to mine I hadn't been in. When I opened the door, I was met with what looked like another bedroom. It was painted a pastel purple color, which was weird. I could tell nobody had been in this room for a long time, if ever. A cute desk sat off to the side, with a rolling chair. There wasn't much in the room besides the desk, other than another small bedside table. A doorway led to a pretty big bathroom and a walk-in closet.

I instantly knew this was the room I wanted to makeover. Knowing that this room wasn't used at all made me feel better, because I was a little hesitant on changing a room of Liam's. Redoing this one wouldn't piss him off as much as me redoing the living room. Grinning, I looked around, putting my hands on my hips. I nodded. I could make this room something cool like my own study, or a good guest room. With my mind made up, I left the room, already thinking of a color for the walls and what needed to be done. I walked into my own room and picked up my phone, dialing Garrett to see if he could take me out shopping.

"Hey, Jenna," he immediately answered.

"Hey, Garrett. I have a favor I kind of need from you," I said, sitting on the edge of my bed, holding my phone.

"Sure, what do you need?"

"Well, I need a ride and someone to take me shopping."

"Didn't you go shopping with Lennon a few days ago?" he asked, sounding confused.

"Oh no, I meant shopping to get paint and stuff. I am going to redecorate a room and need to get supplies and stuff. Could you possible drive me and come help?"

"Does Mr. Stanford know about this?"

"Uh…" I trailed off. "No."

I heard him chuckle through the phone. "I'll come help, but I won't be there for at least twenty minutes or so."

"That's okay. I still need to shower and get dressed. Thank you, Garrett." Saying bye for now, I hung up and headed to go shower. If I were like most girls, twenty minutes to get showered and dressed wouldn't be long enough, but I could get ready in ten. I didn't wear much makeup anyways, so that was one less step. Plus, I usually just brushed my hair and let it air dry.

Quickly washing my hair and body, I turned off the water and stepped out about five minutes later. I dried off and looked in the mirror. I noticed I appeared slightly different than I did before moving here. My cheeks had a healthy glow and a slight tan. My body looked fuller instead of the unhealthy weight I had been before. Being able to eat three heavy meals daily had done me some good, and I looked healthy but not overweight. My green eyes had more life in them, not like the dull color they'd been before. Everything about me looked different, but not at the same time.

The longer I stared at myself, I couldn't help but wonder what Liam saw in me to make this deal. I wasn't close to being as pretty as the other girls I bet he had been with. With a face and body like his, there was no way he didn't have supermodels as girlfriends. I was so average with plain blonde hair, green eyes, and an okay body. That must be why he can't look at me without hate, without glaring. Maybe it's because he knew I was too ugly to be by his side, that no one would believe this. I knew I wasn't his first choice, and the thought didn't really hurt. If I were in his shoes I wouldn't choose me, to be honest. No exceptional good looks, smarts, and too much baggage. I would have definitely looked for someone else.

Starting to depress myself, I pushed all thoughts of Liam to the back of my mind and went to get dressed. With only less than ten minutes until Garrett arrived, I need to get going. Grabbing a pair of blue jeans with a rip in one of the knees and an old black tank top, I also slid on a my old pair of black converse before going to brush my hair again. After brushing my hair and my teeth, I put on a little mascara and called it good. My blonde hair hung down my back in loose waves, and my green eyes stood out a little more with the mascara. Smiling at my reflection, I collected my bag and cell phone before heading out the room to see if Garrett had arrived.

As I walked into the living room and past a window, I saw the black sedan pull into the

149

driveway. I opened the front door and headed to the car, making sure the door was behind me. I still hadn't gotten a key to the house and was glad it locked two minutes after it was shut. Without waiting for Garrett to get out of the car, I opened the passenger's side door and slid into the seat.

"Hey." I grinned over at him. Knowing that I was getting out and actually doing something made me happier than I had been earlier. Just sitting around locked inside was making me weird.

"What's up with you today? You're happy," Garrett said, looking at me with a raised eyebrow. I noticed today he was wearing a pair of blue jeans and a red and black plaid shirt with the sleeves to his elbows. His brown hair was styled into a small front mohawk. He looked really good today. If this were any other situation, I probably would be blushing and peeking at him from the corner of my eyes. He was cute, in a boy-next-door type of way.

"What, I can't be happy?" I questioned, looking at him.

"You, happy? No."

"Hey!" I punched his shoulder. "I can be happy whenever I want," I said, folding my arms across my chest. Garrett grinned at me before turning to the front and starting driving down the driveway to the street.

"So where are we going?" he asked a few minutes later.

"Some kind of hardware store that would have paint, paintbrushes, a tarp for the ground, stuff like that," I said, shrugging.

"Okay. So why all the paint equipment? Painting

something?"

"Yeah, I found an empty room/office that I am going to remodel. I need something to do," I stated.

"Does Liam know about this?"

"Nope, and I couldn't care less if he did." I had already made up my mind that I was going to do this, whether Liam wanted me to or not. It was going to be kind of hard, but I wanted a challenge.

"I hope you know that if he asks me, I will tell him. He is my boss, after all." I rolled my eyes at him. Liam asking about me? Now that was hilarious.

"Trust me, he won't ask." During the rest of the ride to Home Depot, we gabbed. Garrett told me about his college classes and how he had so much homework. Hearing about that didn't make me feel bad about not going anymore. I hated homework in school. He knew about me meeting Liam's family and asked how that went. When I told him about Liam's behavior, he just shrugged. He didn't really know him other than what was put on the internet, magazines, and the news.

We pulled up to the store a little bit later, and I motioned for Garrett to follow me.

"You want me to come with you?" he asked, getting out of the car.

"Duh. Why else would I bring you? You're going to help me decide on a color." I grinned and headed to the entrance. Garrett reluctantly followed me.

"Jenna, you know you are so weird, right? "Garrett asked, walking alongside me as we headed toward the paint section.

"What gave you the impression that I was normal?" I fired right back, turning and raising an eyebrow at him.

"Touchè." We grinned at each other and came to a stop in front of a huge wall of different colors of paint. "It's going to take a while to choose a color," Garrett commented.

"Maybe I'm actually thinking of a certain one." I walked over to a row of reds. "I was thinking a red. What do you think?"

"It's not even my room. Why do I have to help?" he said, basically whining at me.

"Because you're my friend and that's what friends do," I stated with my hands on my hips.

"Fine, a red would look good." Rolling my eyes, I turned back to the colors, grabbing a few that ranged from bright red to an almost brown.

"Whoa, look at that hot girl over there!" Garrett suddenly whispered in my ear. I looked up at him and followed his eyes toward a girl standing there with another guy, talking about something. Suppressing an eye roll, I turned back to Garrett.

"Sorry, dude, but she's taken." I patted his arm.

"You don't know that."

"Garrett, they are holding hands," I pointed out, gesturing to their hands intertwined.

"Technicalities." He waved me off. Chuckling, I looked down at my hands.

"Okay, I like these two. Which one?" I held out a deep rusty red color and a little brighter one toward him. "I don't want something too bright or to dark." He sent me a look but glanced down at them.

"The darker one." Grinning, I nodded.

"Okay, now what?" I looked around.

"Have you never done this before, Jenna? You have to get a worker to mix the paint." Okay, I should have thought about this a tad more instead of diving in headfirst. But that was why I brought Garrett along.

"Okay, onward, my noble steed!" I pointed my finger forward.

"You are so fucking weird," Garrett muttered under his breath. Grinning, I followed after him. After we tracked down several employees, someone finally was able to help us. The guy asked me how much I needed, if I wanted a glossy finish, etc. I stared at him, confused, not knowing what he was talking about. Thankfully Garrett cut in, answering them for me. I smiled thankfully up at him, and we headed to get paintbrushes while the paint mixed.

"You really should have thought this through," he commented.

"I know, and thank you for helping me. It probably wasn't the smartest idea," I admitted, looking at all the different brushes.

"You're welcome, and yes it wasn't the smartest idea. But, if you want, I can help you." He leaned down and grabbed some brushes.

"Yes, thank you!"

Fifteen minutes later, we finally got all the things we needed. Armed with paintbrushes, tarps, tape, and paint, we went and checked out. Thankful that Liam put money in my account, I swiped my card before leaving with Garrett.

"Are you going to paint right away when you get home, or tomorrow?"

"Maybe later this afternoon. I mean, it's only ten." I shrugged. "It's probably going to take a while to tape the room off, though."

"If you do it this afternoon, I won't be able to help. I have class at noon," Garrett said, shooting me an apologetic look.

"That's okay. If I decide to wait until tomorrow, I'll text you so you can come and help. Class comes first." I shot him a smile. I was really glad I had someone like Garrett as my driver. He was nice, smart, cute, and made a great friend. After helping me bring everything inside, Garrett had to leave to go to class. I grabbed something quick for an early lunch and ate while thinking over everything I had to do for the room.

Deciding to start taping the room like Garrett said to, I washed my dishes and left the kitchen. I wasn't too worried about Liam coming home and seeing the room. I bet I would have it finished by the time he even thought about coming home. I started taping off what I could before standing in the middle of the room. Okay, this was going to be a lot harder than I originally thought. I had only the lower half of the walls taped off because I couldn't reach any higher, and the desk was in the way and was too heavy for me to move.

Yeah, this was not as easy as I thought it would be.

***

Liam

"Sir, Mr. Mathews is here," my receptionist, Mary, said over the intercom.

"Send him in," I replied. Leaning back in my chair, I turned and looked outside my window. I had the second best office in the building, my father having the first. My window overlooked the busy streets of New York, but in the distance you could see the river running its course through certain parts of town. Nowadays, this place was more of my home than my actual home. I'd spent many nights here working late when I didn't feel up to driving home.

I wasn't this busy at work in the beginning, but now my father was slowly giving me more duties before he passed the head CEO position to me. Work just kept piling higher and higher every day. There were other CEOs and workers that helped with some of it, but sometimes it wasn't enough. You wouldn't think running and owning hotels would be so hard, but it was.

"Liam, my boy," a familiar voice said, making me turn toward the door. In walked one of my father's most trusted partners, Brian Mathews. He and my father have been by each other's side for many years. Brian was always the one to make sure everything was going smoothly and things got done correctly. I'd known him practically my whole life and considered him my second father. He had salt and pepper-colored hair and a pair of kind brown eyes. He was my father's age, fifty-seven.

"Brian," I greeted him, standing up and coming

around my desk. He shook my hand and pulled me into a hug. "What are you doing here? I just saw you three weeks ago," I said, gesturing for him to take a seat.

"This isn't a business call. I heard from your parents that you are engaged. How the hell did that happen?" he asked, smirking at me. "Last I heard, you were off serious relationships and were going to live the bachelor lifestyle for a while."

"It's fairly recent."

"I didn't know you were dating anyone this seriously."

"I kept her a secret. I wanted to see where we were going and didn't want anything to get in the way of it. You know the press and everyone else would have made a big deal out of nothing. It would have made her run away," I lied.

"If your face didn't run her away, then I don't know what would." He laughed, grinning at me. I shook my head at him but smiled. "When will I be able to meet your lovely fiancé?" *Lovely? More like weird and complicated.* "If I had known you were introducing her to your parents, I would have come over."

"Soon, I think."

"From what I hear, she is a looker and very nice. I hope you will have her by your side at the Annual Benefit this Friday. I bet everyone will be dying to meet her." I had forgotten about the Benefit completely. The idea of taking Jenna and having everyone stare at her was not all that appealing. I knew the people who attended those events. They would tear Jenna apart immediately. Everything about her screamed lower class and that she didn't belong at an event like that.

"I don't know. We haven't even told anyone else besides my parents yet," I said.

"Liam, everyone will find out eventually, whether you want them to or not. It's better to do it yourself, before others do it for you."

"You are right." It was true. The moment anyone got wind of my engagement to Jenna, they would be on us like vultures. They would try to find out where Jenna had been, what she did for a living, who her parents where, and, of course, rumors would fly faster than the fall of Rome. People would make up the worst things about Jenna marrying me for money or fame, how she was some spoiled little rich girl who wanted to take over my business, or even that she was pregnant with my child. Whatever people wanted to say, they would. It was better to be on top of it before anything like that could happen. Jenna and I needed to announce it ourselves and in a big way.

"I better get going, son. I have a meeting at noon to take care of. Tell that fiancé of yours I can't wait to meet her." Brian stood up, interrupting my thoughts. Smiling at him, I hugged him goodbye before he left my office. I sat back down heavily in my seat, rubbing my forehead. This deal was a lot harder than I originally thought. *Jenna and I have a lot of work to do to before the Benefit on Friday.*

As it was nearing noon, I figured I'd better go home and warn Jenna and talk to her sooner rather than later. With practically all my work done, I told my receptionist to take any of my calls for the next two hours, as I would be out. I'd been at work since early that morning, so I'd gotten everything completed early. Ever since Jenna moved in, I had been staying at the office later, or all day for that matter. I didn't want to go home and have to deal with her questions and silent stares. I didn't know what was sadder: that I didn't want to be home with my fake fiancé or that I'd rather be at work.

Getting in my car, I drove home thinking about how angry Jenna would get at my news and at the idea of Lennon teaching her how to act. Lennon knew just as well as I did that you had to act a certain way around snotty rich people. If you didn't, then you were immediately picked on until you couldn't take anymore and had to leave. A girl like Jenna would be picked apart in minutes. Pulling into the garage, I slid out of my Audi and headed inside. The moment I stepped through the door, I heard a loud voice down the hallway.

"You little bitch, you are supposed to be helping me!" I heard Jenna saying. *Who is she talking to?* "You have to move! Ugh!" Confused, I headed toward the sound. Grunts reached my ears, and the sound of huffing. *Sounds like she's having sex.*

Coming to a stop in front of my spare room, my eyebrows flew up. Pushing and pulling the desk I put in there a while ago was Jenna. The room was scattered with tarp, with a few paint cans and brushes, and a ladder off in the corner. Jenna was dressed in a pair of worn pale blue skinny jeans that did very well for her ass, and they had a few rips in them by the knees. She was wearing a tight black tank top that had a few splatters of red paint on it.

Her blonde hair was pulled onto the top of her head with a few strands falling out and sticking to her sweat-covered neck and forehead. She grunted, pushing what looked to be all her weight against the desk, trying to move it.

The walls were outlined with blue masking tape, and a few spots had red paint. Turning my head to my right, outside by the door was the mattress leaning against the wall. When I looked back at Jenna, I watched her as she grunted and huffed, not making any progress. *What the hell is she doing?* I stared at my fake fiancé, wondering why I really did choose her.

Chapter Thirteen

Jenna

After pushing and pulling that stupid desk, I finally gave up when it only moved an inch. Panting, I leaned against it and wiped my forehead. *I really need to get in shape.* A clearing of a throat made me look over toward the door. Standing there was Liam, staring at me like I had lost my mind. His eyebrows were raised, and his arms were folded across his chest. I looked around the messy room and bit my bottom lip, looking back at him. I gulped, anxious to see if he was going to yell at me.

"What are you doing?" he asked, pushing off the wall and walking into the room. He turned to me, waiting for my answer.

"Uh, redecorating?" I supplied, watching him move.

"Why this room and not your own?"

"I liked all the colored walls in the other rooms but not this one, so I decided to repaint this one. That's okay, right?" I asked.

"Sure. It's too late now anyways to say no." He shrugged at me. Even though that wasn't much of a yes or a no, I felt relieved.

"What are you doing home?" I wiped my sweaty hands on my jeans, looking at him. Seeing him dressed all fancy, then me standing there sweaty in a pair of old torn jeans and a tank, made me feel dirty and small.

"I need to discuss some things with you."

"Okay, um, can I get a glass of water first?" With just a nod from him as a response, I squeezed past his big frame and headed toward the kitchen. I already knew whatever Liam wanted to discuss with me wasn't something I was going to like. Come to think of it, whenever Liam wanted to "talk" to me, I didn't like it. Or it got me deeper into the hole I'd dug for myself.

Getting a glass of water and gulping the whole thing down in minutes, I turned around and almost crashed into Liam. He had been standing right behind me, watching me drink. I had already come to terms with the fact that I had to do whatever was asked of me, whether I wanted to or not. I was going to take everything in stride and go along with what Liam wanted to discuss.

"What did you need to talk about?" I asked, leaning against the counter.

"You have to listen to everything I say before getting mad, okay?" Liam asked, looking at me weirdly.

"Okay…" I was starting to actually get nervous.

"This Friday is my company's Annual Benefit, and you are coming along with me." *Okay, that isn't so bad.*

"Okay, I can do that," I started to say, but Liam stopped me.

"That's not all. I am going to need Lennon to teach you some of the basics before we go."

"The basics?" Did Liam think I didn't know how to act properly or something?

"How to eat, talk, and walk."

"You think I don't know how to eat, walk, or talk properly?" I asked, feeling myself getting angry. "You think of me as some poor girl who practically doesn't know the basics of life."

"Jenna, no, I didn't say that," he protested, taking a step toward me, but I took one back.

"Just because I grew up in a home with no parents doesn't mean I don't know how to act, Liam," I bit out angrily.

"I am not saying you don't know how, Jenna. I know these people. They will find anything to pick on so they can tear you apart! I am trying to help you get ready to face these people, because if you're not, they will get their claws in you and not let go." He glared down at me, his face hard. "I know you know how to act civil and proper. I am just trying to help. I told you before to not get angry until I was done."

"Yeah, 'cause that's easy to do when someone insults you," I shot back sarcastically.

"Don't push my patience, Jenna," he growled at me. Rolling my eyes at him, I put my hands on my hips.

"Anything else you want to insult me with, or can I get back to what I was doing?" I asked.

"Jenna."

"Fine. Anything else you would like to talk about, my dear fiancé?" I asked in a sweet voice. He rolled his eyes at me but responded.

"Since you will be attending the Benefit with me, this week we will have to come out that we are engaged."

"As in, we take pictures and post them on Facebook or something?"

"Yes, but instead of Facebook we send it into the newspaper." He nodded. I ran my hand down my face, thinking of all this new information.

Okay, this isn't so bad. I just have to do those stupid lessons with Lennon about etiquette and then take engagement photos with Liam. No big deal. I can do this. The "I can do this" mantra was starting to be my life quote or something lately. *Take it all in stride, Jenna.* Taking a deep breath, I nodded at Liam.

"Okay, that sounds good. Are you going to hire a photographer soon so we can take the photos sometime this week?" I asked once I had my feelings under lock and key. He seemed taken aback by my sudden change of mood and my willingness.

"Uh, yeah, I'll call today," he said, looking at me weirdly.

"Sounds good. Let me know when we will be taking them and when I need to meet with Lennon." As I spoke, I almost didn't even recognize my voice, for how calm it was. *You know what? Maybe I should consider being an actor. I could be very good at it.*

"Okay, I—"

"I'd better get back to redecorating." Without waiting for a response, I moved past Liam and headed back to the room. *I handled that pretty well, I must say.* Mentally patting myself on the back, I looked around the room. I needed something to do for a little bit to get my mind off of Liam.

Even though I couldn't move the desk, I grabbed a paintbrush and worked on opening the paint can. Squatting down, I dipped the tip of the brush in the red paint and headed to the wall. Having no idea what to do, I just started painting up and down in the middle of the wall. I formed a little square, and I smiled, glad at the color. It easily covered the light purple on the walls. Once I ran out of paint on my brush, I grabbed my cell phone. I put it in the corner and scrolled through my music. Last week, during my boring days, I'd bought music from iTunes. I now had about forty songs and I wanted more, but I wouldn't believe how much money music actually was. Clicking on a Taylor Swift song, I turned up the volume and got back to painting. "Bad Blood" played throughout the room, and I hummed along with it.

With the music playing, I didn't hear Liam come into the room until I felt a hand brush against my forearm. Jumping, I whirled around and saw him standing next to me, now clad in a pair of blue jeans that had holes in it like mine and a light grey shirt that hugged his upper body. He had the other paintbrush in his hand, swiping up and down along with me. Surprised, I stood there, staring at him helping me paint. I never would have thought he would.

"Are you going to paint or just stare at me?" he asked, still facing the wall. Blushing, I turned back around, moving my brush. Even though there was music playing, things between us were awkward. We were silent for a few minutes, the only sounds being the music and the sound of our paintbrushes against the wall.

"Aren't you supposed to be at work?" I asked.

"I took the day off," he said simply.

"Wow that was quite the answer. I don't know if I'll ever get you to shut up," I replied sarcastically. "Can't you say more than one-word sentences?"

"I could, but I don't want to. See? That wasn't one word," he retorted.

"Six whole words! Is the world ending?" I looked at him with widened eyes.

"Haha, aren't you the joker?" He fake laughed at me.

"Look at you, being almost sarcastic. Who knew you had it in you?" I grinned at him, dipping my brush back in the paint.

"Well, there are a lot of things you don't know about me." *And whose fault is that?* I clamped my lips shut, not wanting to say anything I shouldn't.

"So, this Benefit thingy. It happens every year?" I asked.

"Yes. It is usually held at one of our hotels, and basically everyone is invited."

"What is it for?"

"The children's hospital. We auction off a few things, make some speeches, everyone talks and hopefully donates," Liam said. He made it seem like it wasn't a big deal, but it was, or at least it was to

165

me. Having a benefit to raise money for the children's hospital was really sweet and caring. I thought it would be some benefit where all the rich people just stood around and donated to some fake fund.

"That is…that is great," I finally said. And to hold the event at their own hotel to save costs. I'd never been to any of the Stanford Hotels, but I knew they were huge and nice.

"I'm not heartless like you think I am, Jenna."

"I never said that you were." *Or at least not out loud.* I heard him scoff next to me. "But it wouldn't hurt to be a little nicer."

"Nice? What is that? I've never heard of it." Looking to my right, I watched him grin at me. He'd never smiled like that at me before, and I felt my heart swell and my knees weaken. He had a gorgeous smile that I knew he never showed anyone but his family. That was his real smile. The other one I'd seen in magazines and on the internet looked more forced. He would only smile with his lips, not showing his teeth, and his blue eyes didn't seem to shine the way they did now. I grinned back at him, feeling happy I had finally made him really smile at me, instead of just frowning.

"And here I thought you went to college. Looks like you really are just a pretty face," I commented, shaking my head at him.

"Who needs smarts when you have a face like mine?" He gestured to his face. A laugh escaped my lips as I grinned at him.

"All you need is a sugar mama now. One who will pay for your plastic surgery later on." I pointed my paintbrush at him, forgetting I had just re-dipped it. It was like everything went into slow motion. Red paint flew off my brush and hit Liam straight in the face. I stared at the mess, trying to hold back my widening grin. I hadn't meant to get paint on him, but I was one of those people who talked with their hands a lot.

"I am so sorry," I said but giggled. His blue eyes narrowed. *Uh oh.* "Liam, whatever is going on in your head, it needs to stop." I took a step back. I was smart enough to know that Liam was going to retaliate. "It was an accident."

"I don't think so." He bent over and put more than half of his brush in the paint. As he pulled it out, I watched as paint dripped off of it onto the tarp-covered floor. *I'm in trouble now.*

"Liam," I warned, putting my hand out. Without any warning, he flicked his wrist and sent red paint flying at me. I didn't have time to move or to cover up as paint hit my tank top and my face. I felt it on my cheeks, nose, and forehead. Looking down, I saw my black tank top had drops of splattered paint all over it. I turned back to look at Liam, and I found he had a triumphant grin across his face. He'd just started a war.

Acting like I was inspecting my tank top, I stepped closer to him. As I tried to act casual, I looked up at him before shooting my arm out and wiping my brush up his shirt and to his neck. Standing back, I looked him up and down and nodded.

"Red is really your color." He growled and lunged at me. I didn't dodge in time, and he swiped his brush along my bare arm, up into my hair. I gasped, looking at him while he smirked at me. I felt my hair and pulled it away to see it covered in red paint. No one messed with my hair. Not caring anymore, I jumped toward the paint can and instead of dipping my brush into it, I dipped my fingers. I whirled around and flicked my fingers at Liam, sending paint toward him. It hit his arms, jeans, and t-shirt.

What happened next came like a tornado. Liam charged toward me, swiping at me with his brush. He then put his hand in the paint, like I had. I turned to run, but a strong arm wrapped itself around my waist, stopping me. I squirmed in his grasp, but it did nothing. A red paint-covered hand came into view, and before I knew it, he was smearing it across my face.

"Now red is your color," Liam whispered huskily into my ear. I tried not to shiver, but my body failed me. He let me go a second later, taking a step away from me. I could feel the paint all over my face and even on my eyelids. Payback time! Running to the paint tin, I dipped my *entire* hand into it. I chuckled and ran to Liam and aimed the paint at his hair and face. Satisfied that his brown hair was covered, I started flicking the extra at his shirt.

"Payback's a bitch!" I grinned evilly.

The next few minutes, Liam and I ran away from each other while we threw paint. Most of the time Liam caught up to me, since his legs were longer than mine. I was covered in red paint, but I couldn't care less. Only a few patches of Liam's grey shirt could be seen, but the rest were covered as well. Both of our arms were lined with red from each other's fingerprints, and from our wrists down we were completely covered from sticking our hands into the paint bucket.

"Jenna," Liam growled, stalking toward me. I giggled, not taking his expression seriously. He looked like he was in the Blue Man Group when they play the drums, causing the paint to fly across their faces.

"Yes?" I asked innocently, taking steps backwards as he got closer to me.

"Get over here."

"How about no?" As soon as he got close enough for me to reach, I laid both of my hands firmly on his chest. He stopped and looked down at my hands, then to me. Grinning, I took my hands away and was rewarded seeing both of my handprints clearly on his shirt. The prints covered his boobs, like I was grabbing them. "I think you have a little something on your shirt," I said. I wiggled my fingers in front of me, giggling.

"My turn," was all he said before taking one big step toward me and wrapping his arms around me. I was pushed against his chest and looked up. His cobalt eyes stared down at me, shining with amusement, red paint splattered by his eyebrows. Since he was so much taller than I was, I had to crane my neck to look up at him. "Now, that's better," he whispered, leaning his head lower to mine. I was confused, but seeing his gaze planted firmly on mine, I couldn't open my mouth. Something about his expression lured me in, and I couldn't stop looking at him. Even covered in paint, he was the hottest guy I had ever seen. I watched as his grin widened, and a firm squeeze of my ass jerked my mind out of its naughty thoughts. Liam stepped back from me, rubbing his hands together. Twisting my body, I looked and saw two big handprints right on my ass. It looked just like marks I'd left on his chest.

"You grabbed my ass!" I said, turning to him.

"So? You grabbed my chest!" he shot back, looking smug. I rolled my eyes but still smiled. In that free moment, I looked around the room. My eyes widened as I took in the walls. Every single purple wall was splattered with red paint. It looked like someone had just walked in, grabbed a paint can, and just flicked it all over them. Not one wall was empty; not even the desk, which had red all over it too. *Well, that was not what I had in mind.* I was about to turn around to show Liam when I felt something drip onto of my head. Looking up, I saw the entire paint can being tilted down on top of my head. I let out a scream and turned around, knocking into Liam's chest just as he dumped the rest of the can of paint. I timed it just right so I hit his chest hard and he lost his footing, tipping backwards as the paint spilled all over both of us.

We toppled over, with me on top of him. My head hit his chin, and he let out a groan. A few pieces of what used to be my blonde hair fell in front of my face, completely filled with red paint and dripping onto Liam's face. Looking down at him, I noticed the paint got on him as well, but not as much as me. We were completely covered. I looked up and stared him in the eyes. I grinned at him, and he grinned back as we started laughing. Since I was on his stomach, his laughter rumbled against me. It was the first time I had heard his laugh, and I wanted to hear more of it. His eyes crinkled, and he threw his head back.

Our laughing was interrupted by a loud clearing of someone's throat. Pausing, we both turned our heads to the doorway. There stood a grinning Lennon, and next to her was a very hot guy. He was tall, maybe six foot two, with short blonde hair, and he was very muscular. The blue shirt he had on stretched across his well-defined chest, looking like it would rip any second. He was staring down at us with a raised eyebrow and an amused look on his face.

"What do we have here?"

Chapter Fourteen

"What do we have here?" the new guy's deep voice asked, laced with amusement.

I turned back to Liam, our lips almost touching. Realizing he was staring at me, waiting for me to get off of him, I scrambled up. In one smooth motion, Liam got up, standing next to me. Lennon and the new guy continued to stare at us and grin, and Lennon had her phone in her hand, pointed at us.

"What are you doing here?" Liam asked, crossing his arms over his chest.

"Well, I heard you were engaged. Which is quite the shock since I'd never even met the girl." the guy said, looking over at me. I felt him looking me over from head to toe.

"Blake, come on, don't be mad," Lennon said next to him, putting her small hand on his bicep. Blake? As in Lennon's crush and Liam's best friend? He looked down at her, and I saw him nod slightly.

"Guess we don't have to ask what you guys have

been doing. You know the paint goes on the wall, right?" Lennon said, gesturing between us. I looked over at Liam and bit back a grin. We looked ridiculous, honestly.

"Jenna started it," Liam said suddenly. I turned to him with my jaw hanging open.

"Hey! I didn't mean to! You technically started it by going after me," I said defensively, turning to point my finger at him.

"You put handprints on my chest!"

"Well, you put handprints on my ass!" I yelled back, turning and showing Lennon and Blake. I heard both of them bust out laughing, which made me look at them with narrowed eyes.

"Don't make me come over there, guy I don't know," I warned, taking a step closer to him. All he did was raise an eyebrow at me before turning back to Liam.

"Well, if you guys are done with your paint war, we came over to see if you wanted to get something to eat for dinner," Lennon said. "But if you want to continue flirting, then by all means, go ahead." I blushed, looking anywhere but at Liam. The only reason I was blushing was because earlier I had bad thoughts when I shouldn't have.

"We weren't flirting," Liam bit out next to me. Peeking over at him, I noticed he wasn't as relaxed as he had been a minute ago. His hands were curling into fists, and his jaw was clenched. My heart sunk. *It was nice while it lasted.* Should have known Liam being nice was too good to be true. "I'm going to go shower." With that, he headed for the door, Lennon and Blake moving far away for

173

him to get by. I stared after him, an unknown feeling entering my chest. The sight of him walking away from me actually hurt.

Jenna, stop! You cannot be getting feelings for Liam. He is never nice to you, and when he does talk to you, it's to berate you. Stop whatever it is you are thinking. There was no way I had feelings for Liam, and if I did, it was only anger. This had just been a moment of weirdness. Liam being nice to me just threw me off. That's all. I just needed to shower and wash off this paint. Then I'd be fine. Looking up, I saw both Lennon and Blake looking at me with odd expressions. Shifting awkwardly from foot to foot, I glanced around.

"I'm just going to…" I trailed off and headed out the door. I quickly made my way to my room so I wouldn't drip paint on the tile. When I shut the door, I went to the bathroom and started the shower. I glanced in the mirror and looked away but ended up doing a double take. My green eyes widened at my reflection. My blonde hair was absolutely covered with red paint, my face was splattered with it, and there was even some running down the side of my jaw. Almost every inch of my bare shoulders, arms, and tank top was covered. I could see why Lennon and Blake were staring at me, as well as Liam.

"This paint better not stain my hair," I said. I turned around and starting pulling off my soiled tank. From the corner of my eye, I could see the reflection of my ass in the mirror. Liam's handprints were the only thing on the back of my blue jeans, and you could clearly see that he'd grabbed it. A ghost of a smile appeared on my lips as I finished stripping. Putting everything on a separate towel I had laid on the ground, I hopped in the shower.

It took me almost five times longer than normal to shower. I had to wash my body and hair three times before the water started to run clear. The red water going down the drain would have scared anyone. People would think I had just come back from killing someone. I couldn't see my hair, but I hoped it wasn't stained. After standing in the shower for a while, I was able to get out. Wrapping a towel around myself, I went to the fogged mirror and wiped it clean. I let out a sigh of relief upon seeing my blonde hair was back to its normal color. My skin was tinged a little pink from me scrubbing at it with soap.

Everything but my underwear was ruined, and I knew I had to throw everything away, maybe even my bra that had some paint on the straps and a little on the cups. I went out to my closet and threw on a clean set of underwear, a bra, black skinny jeans, and a grey shirt with an anchor on it that hung off my shoulder. Going back to the bathroom, I grabbed my bad clothes, holding them away from my body. I glanced down at my jeans and bit my bottom lip, pulling them out from my hands. Something inside of me wanted to keep them for some reason. Setting them on the edge of my bathtub to dry, I left my bathroom and my room.

I padded barefoot to the kitchen in search of a bag to put my clothes in. I stood at the entrance, seeing everyone already in there whispering intensely with one another. I knew they were probably talking about me. As much as I wanted to eavesdrop and hear what they are saying, I cleared my throat. Sometimes it was better to not hear what people say about you; plus, it wasn't like I hadn't heard any of it before. I'd heard enough bad things said about me that could make me cry for days on end.

Once I cleared my throat, they all snapped their heads toward me. Rolling my eyes, I walked into the kitchen, going to the cabinet under the sink for a garbage bag. Awkwardly, I opened the bag with one hand and shoved my clothes in with the other.

"Jenna, this is Blake Williams," Lennon said, gesturing to him. "He's who I was talking about a week ago." Up close, I could now see he had a pair of pretty light blue eyes.

"Hi, nice to meet you," I said, sending him an awkward wave. I hated meeting new people. I didn't know if I should shake their hands, hug them, or just stand there like an idiot. I usually opted for standing there like an idiot.

"Blake, this is Jenna Howard, as you already know."

He gave me a nod in greeting.

"So you're the one who is engaged to my annoying friend. What made you do it?" Blake asked.

"Definitely not his personality," I said before thinking. Lennon's laugh echoed through the kitchen while Liam just glared at me. I held back a smirk before opening my mouth.

"So, dinner? I'm starving."

176

"Where do you want to go?" Lennon asked, looking at each of us.

"Probably nowhere expensive, since Jenna can't afford it," Liam shot at me, his blue eyes back to being expressionless and cold. The comment hurt more than I let on. I didn't know what had happened to Liam when Blake and Lennon had made themselves known. We were fine playing around and laughing at each other. It seemed like whenever someone else was around, he acted differently—colder and more rude. It seemed Liam just had to say something rude to me at every possible moment. Schooling my face so it was calm, I tried not to let my emotions show. I'd gotten pretty good at doing so over the years. I was starting to think it would literally kill Liam if he was nice to me.

"You don't remember, sweetie?" I asked in a fake sweet tone, with an intentionally confused face. "You gave me money on a credit card...so I think I can afford it." I plastered on a fake smile. "Let me grab some shoes." With that, I headed back to my room. Muttering under my breath, I grabbed a new pair of black Converse I'd gotten at the mall the other day. With my bag swung across my shoulder and my phone in my pocket, I went back to the kitchen. Liam really did know how to push my buttons.

"Let's all ride in one car," was the first thing Lennon said the moment I walked through the door. Before I could even ask what we were doing, she had her arm hooked through mine, dragging me down the hall toward the garage; the two boys

177

followed behind us quietly. Lennon didn't even wait for them as she dragged both of us toward the Jeep Rubicon at the far side of the garage.

"I just love this car," she said, jumping into the back seat.

"I haven't been in it yet, but I love Jeeps," I said, sliding in next to her.

"Let me guess, you're always in the Audi," she said. I nodded just as the guys opened the doors and got in.

"Lenn, why did you pick the Jeep out of all the cars?" Blake practically whined, looking over his shoulder at her.

"I wanted to ride in something different, so sue me." She stuck her tongue out at him immaturely. "Let's go to Rick's Pizzeria." I watched Liam roll his eyes in the rearview mirror, but he did what she asked and backed out of the driveway. I could tell she was the one who told everyone else what to do.

The whole ride to Rick's Pizzeria, Lennon made conversation between everyone, trying to lighten the atmosphere. Her and Blake talked about random topics such as which phone device was better, the iPhone or Samsung Galaxy, to what pizza topping was better. I studied Blake the whole ride, and from the way he interacted with Lennon I was starting to like him. He was a big guy, probably worked out every day of the week, but when it came to his friends he seemed like a big softie. At first I thought he didn't like me, but it seemed like he got over the fact no one told him about Liam and me.

About fifteen minutes later, Liam pulled the car into a parking lot of a cute little place. It was an old brick building that was set between two bigger buildings that were probably businesses. We all jumped out of the car and headed inside. The moment I stepped through the door, the smell of homemade pizza hit me straight in the face. I hadn't had anything to eat in hours, and the smell of it and garlic bread was making my stomach grumble. I could tell it was a family-owned place. Black and white pictures covered the walls, as well as colored ones. The red walls were inviting, as was the atmosphere. The place seemed pretty busy as we waited to be seated. A few minutes later, a plump woman came up and grinned at Liam, Blake, and Lennon.

"Liam, Blake, Lennon, I haven't seen you in a while," the woman said in a pretty thick Brooklyn accent. She hugged them all and kissed them on their cheeks before coming to a stop in front of me. "And who is this lovely lady?" She suddenly grabbed and hugged me tightly to her. I looked over her shoulder at Liam, but he just ignored me.

"I'm Jenna, just a friend," I said once she let me go and stared at me.

"Mmhmmm." She looked at me one more time before turning around and grabbing menus. "Right this way." I trailed behind everyone as we were led toward the back of the restaurant to a booth. With Lennon next to Blake, I had no choice but to sit next to Liam.

"How about a large three-topping pizza?" Blake asked, not even glancing at his menu. Looking around, I noticed none of them were. "And wings." Next to Blake, Lennon rolled her eyes, but she was smiling. Before I could even answer, the same woman came over to the table to take our order. In less than a second, Blake rattled off the order and the lady left. It was pretty clear they had been here a lot. "So, Jenna, tell me about yourself. Liam has told me nothing about you," Blake said, putting his hands on the table and leaning toward me. *No surprise there.*

"There's really nothing to tell. I'm not an interesting person," I said, shrugging. "How about you? I don't know anything about you, either." I tried to switch the topic. I was not in the mood to talk about myself tonight.

"Blake works with his father; they own a big construction company," Lennon butted in before Blake could answer.

"Wow, that's impressive."

"Soon I will own the company here in New York."

"Sounds like you guys have a good business." I shot him a smile. Blake opened his mouth to answer but was cut off when a pitcher of beer was put in front of us. Before the lady could leave, I asked for a glass of water before turning back to three sets of eyes staring at me.

"You don't drink?" Blake asked, pouring beer into three glasses.

"No, not really. Plus, I'm too young." He sent me a weird look, but I let it go. Was it weird that a nineteen year old didn't like alcohol or something?

Conversation for the next little bit was light with Liam, Lennon, and Blake talking to one another. I added in a couple of times but mostly sat back and listened to them talk about work and reminisce about their childhoods together. I felt out of place among the three of them and couldn't help but feel I shouldn't be here. I should have just stayed home and made myself something to eat instead. Liam wouldn't look in my direction, and when he did it was a frown or a glare when I added to the conversation. I watched as Lennon was hanging onto Blake's every word, clearly smitten with him. Blake was laughing and smiling over at her with a wide white grin, completely ignorant of the looks Lennon was giving him. When I looked at both of them, I knew they would make a cute couple and that I would have to be Cupid for them soon. The three of them had a bond that I knew no one could break, and I was impeding on it.

Watching them talk and laugh made me jealous. I'd never had a group of friends like that. The two friends I had in high school were closer to each other than they were with me, and I had been fine with that. You would think that during high school I would want to have close friends, but I didn't. I was fine being alone until recently; lately I'd wanted someone to be around, someone to talk to. I missed Candy and Sophia more than ever, what with being cooped up in a big house by myself and that making me antsy and lonely. Sitting here listening to them talk really made me feel lonely. I didn't belong with them.

The longer I sat there, the worse I started to feel. I kept getting lower and lower in the booth, trying to act invisible. After saying something in the conversation and hearing Liam scoff at me, I knew I had to leave. I couldn't sit there any longer listening to them acting like I wasn't there. I knew when I wasn't wanted. When there was a break of silence, I sat up.

"Hey, guys, I think I'm going to go," I said quickly before losing my confidence.

"What, why?" Lennon asked, looking at me. I felt Blake's and Liam's eyes on me as well.

"I...I don't feel so good. I'm sorry, but please stay and eat." I forced a smile, sliding out of the booth.

"No, it's okay. We can take you home," Blake said, making a move to stand up.

"No! No, stay, really. I'm fine." I shot my hand out onto his arm, stopping him. They didn't need to leave just because I was.

"At least let Liam take you back," Lennon reasoned. I looked over and saw Liam with his jaw clenched and a dark look on his face.

"It's fine. I'll see you guys later, though. It was nice meeting you, Blake." Nodding at them, I turned and walked away from the table before they could say anything else. I knew Liam wasn't happy about me being there, and it would make him angrier if he had to take me home. I'd just get a taxi. Swallowing the lump in my throat, I gripped the handle on my bag and made my way to the front door. I ignored my rumbling stomach and pushed open the door.

What I didn't expect was to be bombarded with flashing lights as soon as I walked outside. People were yelling, and the clicking of cameras reached my ears and eyes, making my duck my head. *Where the hell did these people come from? They must think I'm somebody else.*

"It's her! It's her!"

Hearing the paparazzi yell that, I jerked my head up, confused. *Me?* The flashing lights from all of their cameras were making me see spots, and my head was starting to hurt. Not caring what they were saying, I tried to push past them, but they wouldn't move. It was like they set up a wall of their bodies, making sure no one got around them.

"Jenna Howard!"

"Jenna, look over here!"

"Why are you at a pizzeria?"

"Where's Liam Stanford?"

"Is it true you are engaged?"

"When is the wedding?"

"Are you just marrying him for his money?"

They all shouted at me, not even stopping for me to answer. I couldn't see past the lights, but I figured there had to be about fifteen reporters. My eyes widened as I heard their questions asking if I was pregnant, where Liam was, why was I dressed like I was, when the wedding was. *How did they know?* Some of the things they were saying were making my eyes tear up.

"I, uh—" I opened my mouth, but nothing came out. I tried to again get through them, but I was just pushed back. I suddenly felt a hard warm thing press against my back before the reporters went crazy, yelling and snapping away at us. Not caring who it was, I turned and pressed my face against them. I could feel my body starting to shake and my tears threatening to spill. A big arm wrapped around my lower back, pulling tight against them. I inhaled and knew it was Liam; the smell of his cologne filled my nose and made me relax a little bit.

"Get out of the way!" Liam yelled above me, holding me against him as he pushed his way through the reporters. I clenched onto his shirt as he tucked me into his side and shoved his way toward the Jeep. The reporters kept shouting questions at us and coming closer until I felt their cameras actually touching my arms. This had never happened to me before, and I was starting to freak. I hated attention and hated being asked such personal questions. Being asked if I was some whore that Liam paid or that I was just a gold digger actually hurt, a lot more than I thought.

Thankfully, a minute later Liam was picking me up and sliding me inside the Jeep. I hadn't even heard him open the door with the cameras clicking and the reporters yelling. He slammed the door shut, and I ducked my head down in my lap. Liam made his way around the car and into the driver's side. Without a single word, he started the car and backed up. I didn't even care in that moment that he could run someone over, and he didn't seem to either; all we wanted to do was get the hell out of here. The windows muffled the shouting, and in a matter of seconds they faded away as Liam drove us far away from the restaurant.

I slumped back against the seat, looking down at my shaking hands in my lap. I gulped, trying to push my tears away. The car was silent as we drove down the street to only God knew where. I wanted to thank Liam, but I didn't know how to say it or what to say. I didn't know that agreeing with Liam would mean paparazzi showing up, suddenly taking pictures.

"Are you okay?" Liam asked, his voice soft. Taken aback, I slowly nodded, not looking at him. Physically I was fine, but emotionally I wasn't. "I didn't know they would find us," he muttered, obviously not thinking I heard him.

"It's okay," I croaked out, peeking out of the corner of my eye at him. He shook his head, his brown hair falling onto his forehead. My hand itched to move it, but I locked both of them together in my lap. I was still surprised Liam actually came after me.

"I'm sorry," he said suddenly, reaching over and grabbing my hand into his. I froze, looking down at our hands then up to him. His warm hand fit perfectly in mine, and I loved the feeling of his in my own. I'd never held a guy's hand before, but holding Liam's felt right. I felt like I wasn't missing something anymore.

"It's okay, Liam," I said softly, still looking at our hands.

"Want to grab something quick to eat?" he asked. At the mention of food, my stomach growled, making me blush. Since I left before the food came and so did Liam, I bet he was hungry too. "I'll take that as a yes."

With his hand still on mine, he shot me a smile and continued driving. He was back to acting nice to me, when only twenty minutes ago he was rude. I wanted to be angry and not go anywhere with him, but the moment he shot me that smile, I knew I wouldn't do any of that. He didn't know it, but he had me in chains. When Liam wasn't an ass, I actually liked him. And even if he was rude, I still looked past it even though I shouldn't. Before I could actually think about it any further or do anything, he pulled up to McDonald's and turned to me with a grin.

Yes, Liam, you had me in chains.

Chapter Fifteen

As we walked into McDonald's, I was hit with the smell of cheap fast food and the sound of kids yelling. It had been a while since I'd been here. The smell of fresh fries filled my nose, making my stomach growl loudly. The place was pretty busy for a Monday, with a few little kids running to the indoor playground and a few teenagers laughing and talking. As I waited in line next to a quiet Liam, a little girl, about seven years old, caught my attention. I watched as she twirled around tables in a bright red shirt that had a heart on it, with a blue and pink tutu around her waist. Her brown hair was in two pigtails, and a giant grin was spread across her face, showing her two front teeth.

I knew I was probably staring at her like a weirdo, but I couldn't help it. I loved how she didn't match and that she didn't care that people were watching her dancing around. A woman, who I assumed was her mother, sat off to the side, smiling fondly at her daughter as she giggled and paraded around. A wave of sadness and jealousy washed over me. The feeling wasn't anything new to me, but it still hurt every time I saw a mother and daughter. Not having a mother around and seeing other girls with theirs always made me feel sad. I didn't have one, and I was jealous because I wanted one. I wanted a mom who I could tell everything to, someone who would look at me like that mother was doing with her daughter, like I was her entire universe. A mom who would be cheering me on no matter what I did and helping me up when I fell.

The older I got, the worse I seemed to feel when I saw things like that. When I was younger, I used to think my mom would come back for me, that I would always have someone there for me. But as I aged, I knew she wasn't coming back and that I was all on my own. You don't realize it, but the older you get the more you need your mom. As a teenager you didn't want anything to do with her, and as the world starts to become bigger and heavier, you need someone there to help with the weight.

When I felt a nudge on my arm, I looked away from the mother and daughter to see that it was our turn to order. Usually the sight didn't bother me so much. Having worked at the diner helped me put a hard shield around myself at the sight of families. Maybe my emotions were already high from the paparazzi, because I could feel my eyes tearing up and my throat tightening. Swallowing the lump in my throat and blinking my eyes rapidly, I got ready to order. While I ordered, I ignored the daggers being sent at me by the girl behind the counter. My head would have two holes in it if her would get heated stares. Not bothering to argue with Liam about paying, I grabbed our cups and walked off, rolling my eyes at the girl.

After getting my drink and handing Liam his, I found us a seat near the back by the window. When Liam took a seat across from me, I looked anywhere but at him. What could I say to him? Thank you for saving me from the paparazzi? Thanks for being a complete ass to me in front of your friends?

"I'm sorry," Liam said suddenly, making me snap my head up to stare at him. I didn't know what he was apologizing for, but I was going to take it either way. It was not everyday he said sorry. That's for sure.

"It's fine."

"I don't know how the paparazzi found out. Lennon and Blake wouldn't tell anyone," he said quietly, almost to himself. Before he had time to think more into it, our order was called. For the next few minutes we ate silently, both of us lost in thought. I stared at Liam while he ate like a complete weirdo, finding him even more attractive as he chewed. *Wow, did I hit my head or something?* "So Blake seemed nice," I commented, tired of the silence between us.

"Yeah, he's a great guy. Takes a little bit to get through his exterior."

Like you? "You didn't have to leave the restaurant because of me," I said a few minutes later.

"Well, Lennon didn't want you walking home by yourself." Wow, and here I thought he did it from the goodness of his heart. Boy was I wrong. "Plus, she kind of threatened me." *Well, at least I know*

Lennon likes me. Rolling my eyes, I stuffed a few French fries in my mouth. Right now I couldn't care less what Liam thought of me eating. The silence between us dragged on until I was halfway through my McNuggets. Then I snapped.

"Liam, you have to talk or something because this silence is killing me. Apologize for being an ass to me and then move on," I snapped at him. The longer we sat there not saying a word, the more angry and agitated I was becoming. Liam needed to man up and say sorry before we could go any further. I was not going to say sorry first; I had nothing to say sorry for.

Liam looked over at me, and for a split second I didn't see the guy I had come to know. Instead, his blue eyes seemed to soften with guilt, and his expression morphed into something other than narrow and cold.

"Sorry," he said so quietly that if I wasn't already leaning toward him, I wouldn't have heard. The moment after he said sorry, his face became emotionless once again, and he was back to the old Liam I had come to know and hate. I could almost see the walls he had built around his heart come down, but he was still shielding himself. I knew that was the only sorry I was going to get. I let out a sigh. Even though he didn't specifically say what he was sorry for, I was going to take it and move on. I really wasn't one to hold grudges, and holding one against Liam would just be futile.

"So what exactly is this benefit thing?" I asked, changing the subject.

"It is kind of like a benefit. Raise money and

send it to children's hospitals all through New York. But it is mostly just a thing where all the upper class people come to show off," Liam answered, sounding bitter toward the end.

"You don't sound too excited about going," I said, taking a sip of my drink. Liam brought a fry to his mouth and angrily chomped down on it.

"No. Snotty rich people showing off how much more money they've got or what new summer house they just got in the Hamptons, definitely not my favorite kind of event to attend."

"Well at least they are donating to the children's hospitals. That's always good," I commented, trying to find a bright side but probably failing. Just from the sound of it, I was already dreading having to go.

"That is the only plus to this event. If I had a choice, I'd rather stay home."

"You mean you don't want to go and talk to people who couldn't care less all the while wearing a fake smile?" I asked sarcastically. "That sounds like a boatload of fun to me."

"You'll fit right in, then." He shot me a smile. I couldn't help but let out a laugh at that. We both knew I would not be the one fitting in; I'd be more of the person who would stand in the corner watching as woman threw themselves at Liam, oblivious that I was his "fiancé".

"Are you sure you want to me go with you?" I asked, hoping he would say no.

"Yes, it will be a good opportunity for us to show up after announcing our engagement later this week." *Damn, there went that plan.* I had actually forgotten about the pictures Liam and I were supposed to take later this week, announcing that we were engaged to everyone. Yep, definitely not looking forward to that.

"It's this Friday, right?"

"Yes." So much to do in just four days. We needed to get our pictures taken, and I needed to take those stupid lessons with Lennon, all before Friday night. Busy week ahead of us. The conversation kind of died after that, leaving us to finish our food in silence, but this time it wasn't uncomfortable. Five minutes later, I stood up, grabbing my garbage with Liam behind me. Sipping on my drink, I followed Liam back to the Jeep and slid inside. I was glad this time there were no people with cameras waiting for us.

"Thank you for coming out after me tonight, Liam, even if Lennon made you. You really saved me from the paps," I said as we started on our way back home. "And, also, thank you for 'helping' me paint the spare room today and not freaking out that I did it without you knowing," I added. For some reason, it felt like a lifetime ago that we were throwing paint at one another, but it had really been just this morning.

"You're welcome. Jenna, I am sorry about saying those rude things to you this afternoon in front of Lennon and Blake. I didn't mean any of it. And I am sorry for being so rude to you as well," Liam said. I held back my wide grin that was threatening to break free. The rest of the ride home was quiet, the radio playing softly throughout the car.

As I was making my way to the kitchen after

arriving home to throw away my drink, the sound of a knock at the front door made me stop. I turned to Liam next to me with a raised eyebrow, wondering who was here. It was seven at night, and I was pretty sure it wasn't Lennon and Blake checking up on us. Liam just shrugged at me, going toward the front door. I quickly stepped into the kitchen and threw my cup away before going to see who was at the door. When I went into the living room, I saw Garrett standing next to Liam.

"Garrett, what are you doing here?" I asked, walking toward him, confused. Why was he here at seven? I knew he had class early tomorrow.

"I was just checking up on you. I called and texted you a while ago and never heard back, so I got worried." I looked down at my bag, where my phone was on silent. After I got changed to go to dinner, I didn't even bother to check my phone.

"I'm sorry I haven't even looked at my phone all afternoon. We just got back from dinner," I said, sending him a guilty look.

"That's okay. I just wanted to know if you needed help painting the room tomorrow," Garrett said, sending me a smile that showed his left cheek dimple.

"You're helping her paint the spare room? I thought I hired you to be a driver," Liam butted in. His voice was low, and he was glaring over at Garrett. I watched as Garrett looked between Liam and me, confused.

"Uh, Jenna asked me this morning if I'd help," he said slowly, looking over at me.

"Well, she doesn't need your help anymore. We

painted it this afternoon."

"Liam—" I started to say, but Garrett cut me off.

"Oh, are you guys doing real couple things now?" he asked, turning to Liam. Even though Liam stood a few good inches above Garrett, my driver seemed to be toe to toe with him. Something in Garrett's tone made me take a step closer to them. Both boys seemed to be having a stare down, and with a grin plastered on Garrett's face, I could tell he was goading Liam on.

"What do you mean 'doing real couple things now'?" asked Liam, his gaze never wavering from Garrett's.

"You guys—" I tried to say but was cut off once again.

"Well, seeing as you aren't a real couple, it's just interesting hearing you're doing things together now," Garrett said, shrugging as if it was no big deal. I hadn't realized that telling Garrett that we weren't really engaged was a bad idea or that Liam would find out. Slowly, Liam turned toward me, his blue eyes hard.

"You told him about our deal?" he ground out. The look he was sending me was making my knees weak, it was not a good weak, and I was suddenly nervous.

"I…uh well…" I tried to come up with the best way to say it, but nothing came out.

"You did!" he yelled suddenly. "Jenna, I specifically told you not to tell *anyone* about this! You signed a contract saying you would not. Good God, Jenna, he is probably the one who told the paparazzi and maybe even the paper!" Liam yelled.

194

"I didn't mean to, Liam! It kind of just slipped out, but Garrett would never do that! He promised me he wouldn't tell anyone," I defended, looking over at Garrett for confirmation. Instead of finding confusion like I thought I would, he was staring at me guiltily. "Garrett, please tell me you didn't!" I turned to him.

"Jenna, I didn't tell them your engagement was a fake. I just told them you were engaged!" I stared at him, shocked that he would even do such a thing. "I swear, Jenna, I didn't tell them it was all fake. They came up to me after I dropped you off this morning, asking me about Liam and who I dropped off at his house. They paid me three grand to tell!" His brown eyes were pleading for me to understand.

"This is why I don't trust people, especially you! Garrett, get the hell out of my house. You're fired!" Liam roared at me, then at Garrett. I was too stunned from Garrett's betrayal that I didn't even flinch as Liam yelled at me. Garrett got the hint that he'd better leave before Liam did something; as he backed away to the door, he kept his gaze on me.

"Jenna, I am sorry. I didn't mean to get you hurt or anything. I thought it was harmless information."

"I swear to God, if you don't leave right now, I will personally make you," Liam growled, taking a step closer to him. Garrett let out a sigh, nodding at him.

"I really am sorry, Jenna. I hope you can forgive me. You have my number if you need me." With one last sad look, he turned and walked out the door. I stared after him, not knowing what to say. I never would have thought Garrett would say anything. The bright side was that he didn't tell the paparazzi my and Liam's relationship was a lie. I just couldn't believe that he would sell me out for money! At that thought, my insides froze. But wasn't I doing almost the exact same thing? I was doing something to get money, just like him. *I'm no better.*

I stood with my back to Liam, awaiting the yelling I knew was coming my way. How was I supposed to know Garrett would go spill to the paparazzi? It wasn't my fault. *It's your fault for trusting someone,* a little voice said in the back of my head. With one last look at the door, I turned around to face Liam. I knew nothing I could do would make any difference with Garrett, and I might as well face Liam now.

"Liam, I—"

"No, Jenna. This whole mess, that will include the newspaper in the morning, is because of you. I told you not to tell anyone about this because someone will find out. Now we have to do damage control before anything else gets out of hand. You should not have opened your big mouth. It seems that whenever you do, something goes wrong," Liam said. His blue eyes were dark, and his mouth was set in a firm line. The way he was talking to me made me feel like I was being scolded. "Who else have you told?"

"No one," I said quietly, feeling small under his gaze. I briefly thought of Sophia but immediately shut that thought down. Out of anyone, she would never tell a soul. Liam stared at me almost like he was waiting for me to crack and say something else.

"You'd better be right, because if I find out anyone else knows, I will make it my personal mission to end you," he threatened. I stared up at him, scared. Liam was making this to be worse than it actually was. They only knew that we were engaged, not about anything else.

"Liam, you are making this to be worse than it is," I said, my voice soft, afraid that if I said anything too loud it would set him off even more.

"Worse than it is? Do you not realize what will happen if people find out I am paying you to marry me? My father's business will crash, my family will be ridiculed, and don't forget breaking my mother's heart."

"I'm sorry. I didn't think he would do anything if I told him."

"That is right. You don't think, Jenna! You only think about yourself and what will happen to you. I seriously can't even stand to be in the same room as you. From now on, you will stay in this house unless I tell you to. Do not even think about leaving, because I will know. You will do everything that I say this week, and if you don't, you are done." His voice was so cold and emotionless I felt my blood freeze. From the way he was looking at me, I knew he was beyond serious. He was like a bear that was waiting to be poked. "Why I chose someone so incompetent, I have no idea. You were definitely a mistake." With that, he turned on his heel and stalked out of the room. I watched after him and jumped when the door to the garage slammed.

"I'm sorry," I whispered to the empty room, wrapping an arm around myself. I was always left alone. I let one tear slide down my cheek before heading to my room. Liam was right. Everything I said or did turned into a mess. Maybe I was a mistake.

Chapter Sixteen

That night, all I did was toss and turn. No matter what I did, I couldn't get comfortable, and I couldn't get Liam's words out of my head. He was right, and that was the problem. The words that were true were the cruelest, because deep down you knew it and it scared you. They were always the words that hurt you the most. I finally gave up around three in the morning, knowing that it was no use to try and sleep. Feeling confined in my room, I threw my sheets off, grabbed a light sweater, and quietly padded to my door. Praying it wouldn't squeak, I opened it and nodded when it didn't. With one place on my mind, I tiptoed down the hallway to the kitchen.

Throwing on my sweater, I opened the back door and headed outside toward the gazebo. The light breeze blew across my bare legs as I made my way around the pool, the glow of the moon guiding me. The air was kind of cold, making me wrap my sweater more tightly around me. A few pieces of hair that had fallen from my messy bun blew in my face.

I finally made it to the gazebo and took a seat on the bench. Pulling my knees to my chest, I wrapped my arms around them. I closed my eyes, breathing in the fresh air, and felt my body finally relax. My mind started shutting down, only concentrating on being outside instead of what happened yesterday. Even though it was three in the morning, I was wide awake.

Opening my eyes, I leaned to my left and looked up at the moonlit sky. Since we were a little outside of the city, I could see some stars above me. Seeing the dark sky only lit by the moon made everything seem so peaceful and mystical. For some odd reason, I had always loved the night more than the daytime. Being dark outside, it is easier to hide your feelings, your demons, and even your thoughts, but during the daytime everything could be seen and picked apart. It was easy shielding yourself at night. When I was younger, I used to climb on the roof of the home and stare at the stars in the middle of the night. I felt safer and peaceful watching the stars twinkle and seeing an airplane slowly make its way across the sky. Even though the next morning I would be tired and barely awake during class, I didn't care.

Leaning my head back against the wood of the gazebo, I closed my eyes again, listening to the sound of crickets and the wind blowing through the yard. I didn't know how long I stayed out there with my eyes closed and slowly drifting off to sleep. The rise of the sun jerked me awake, and I groggily sat up, looking around. My back was stiff from being in the same position all night. With a small groan, I stood up and stretched, hearing my body crack. It was probably only six in the morning, and I was more than happy to head back to bed. With my eyes half-closed, I made my way back to the house.

The sound of glass clinking reached my ears as I stepped onto the patio. I knew Liam was up, but I had no intention of seeing and talking to him unless told otherwise. Not bothering to even knock so I don't scare him, I opened the door and walked into the kitchen. I didn't miss the surprise and confused look on his face as I walked by him, half-asleep. He stood frozen, watching me with a cup of coffee in his hand. Without a glance in his direction, I walked out of the kitchen and to my room. Without taking my sweater off, I plopped down on the bed and was out in seconds.

***

The sound of my cell phone ringing brought me out of my dreamless sleep. I groaned, turned over, and blindly reached for my phone, my eyes still closed. After almost dropping it twice, I finally grabbed it and brought it to my ear.

"Hello?" I croaked, my voice deep with sleep. *Man, I sound like I smoke three packs a day.*

"Jenna, where have you been? I have been calling and texting without an answer from you," a familiar high-pitched voice yelled into my ear.

"Candy—" I started to say, but she cut me off.

"What happened to calling me every day?" I sat up and ran my free hand down my face.

"I'm sorry, Candy. Things have just been crazy," I said, apologizing and feeling bad that I hadn't talked to her or Sophia in a while.

"Well, you are going to make it up to me. I'm coming over," she said. With that, my eyes snapped fully open.

"Wait, what? You coming here?"

"Yes, I need you to watch Sky for a little bit. I have a test to take in an hour and then work until nine. You can make it up to me this way. Plus she's been missing you," Candy said. "What is your address?"

"Candy, I don't think—"

"I am coming over. Now, what is your address?" she asked in a firm tone. Sighing, I told her the address and hung up. Knowing Candy, I knew she would be here soon, so I reluctantly got up and made my way to my bathroom. I needed a cold shower to wake me up, so I stripped out of my sweater and my PJs. Seeing the clock from the corner of my eye, I saw it was ten. With only a few hours of sleep in me, I knew this day was going to be a long one.

I stood in the shower for a good ten minutes before I made myself get out. With pruned fingers, I dried my body off and started to feel more awake. A cold shower always did the trick. I quickly got dressed in a pair of old shorts and a t-shirt, putting my hair in a high ponytail. I grabbed my phone and left my room. I didn't make it far, as the doorbell rang. Getting excited to see Candy and her little girl, Sky, I grinned, walking quickly to get the door. When I opened it, I was instantly thrown back by a little body running into me. Sky wrapped her arms around my waist and grinned up at me, showing me one of her two front teeth. Her blonde hair was up in two pigtails, and her identical blue eyes, which were like her mom's, sparkled up at me. She was dressed in a pink dress that had a unicorn on it, and black leggings underneath.

"Wenna!" she yelled up at me. My grin widened as I leaned down and scooped the four year old in my arms. I loved how she said my name with a "W" instead of a "J".

"Sky!" I said, placing a kiss to her cheek. "I've missed you." Instead of saying anything, she kissed my cheek in return and played with my hair in my ponytail. She'd always had a weird fascination with my hair. "Candy—" I turned to say but stopped. She stood outside the door, staring straight past me. I knew she was surprised by where I was living when only three weeks ago I was in some shack of a place.

"You live here?" she all but yelled. "You will be telling me everything." With that, she walked past me and into the house. Rolling my eyes, I shut the door with one hand and followed her. I was only a few feet inside when Sky wanted down. The moment her feet touched the ground, she was running to the TV and staring up at it.

"You got yourself a sugar daddy, didn't you?" Candy asked, turning on me with a wide grin on her face.

"What? No!" I said. Of course she would think that, but in a way it was kind of true.

"Oh, okay, like a house like this doesn't belong

to someone with a lot of money. Hate to break it to you, Jenna, but only old guys have a lot of money." I resisted the urge to tell her Liam wasn't old. *Let her think what she wants.*

"So you need me to watch Sky for a few hours?" I asked, changing the topic. Thankfully, Candy didn't press anymore on the subject and nodded.

"Yeah. I have a test for hair school in twenty minutes, then work right after. Is it okay that she stays here with you?" I had forgotten Candy was going to hair school during the day and worked at the club at night. Honestly, she was someone I could see doing hair. She only had a few more tests to take and then she would be certified.

"It is totally fine. I wasn't planning on doing anything today anyways." *Yeah, and you are on house arrest.* "I've missed hanging out with Sky," I said, shooting her a smile as she walked around the living room.

"Thank you, Jenna. I will be here right after work, around nine. Here is her blanket, stuffed animal, and her PJs," she said, handing me a bag I didn't even notice she was carrying. "Baby, come give me a hug and a kiss before I leave." I watched as Sky ran over to her mom and gave her a tight hug and a kiss. I smiled sadly at the sight. "Be good for Jenna, okay? Do as she says, and I will see you tonight." Candy kissed the top of her head before standing up.

"Thank you again, Jenna." She gave me a quick hug and apologized for leaving before opening the door and leaving. *Okay, what to do to entertain a four year old? I bet Liam doesn't have any board games.* "Sky, what would you like to do today?" I asked, taking a seat on the couch. She jumped up next to me and moved her legs back and forth, her feet not touching the ground.

"I want ice cream!" At the mention of food, my stomach rumbled softly. The way Sky was sending me puppy dog eyes, I immediately caved even though it was only eleven in the morning.

"Ice cream, you say? I don't think you want it quite enough," I said, rubbing my chin and hiding my grin at the look Sky had on her face.

"Wenna, I want ice cream! Very badly," she whined. I leaned my head down so we were eye to eye and looked at her. For some reason, she found that the funniest thing and started giggling in my face. I couldn't help but let my smile slip out.

"Okay, we will get ice cream."

"Yay!" With that, she jumped up and ran around the living room. I was about to stand up when I realized I had no ride to get us to get ice cream and Liam would get mad if I left. Since I couldn't drive, it wasn't like I could borrow that car. Biting my bottom lip, I hesitantly grabbed my phone. I stared down at the five contacts on my phone. I couldn't call Garrett. I wasn't planning on talking to him for a while, as I needed to cool off before I did. With him and Sophia out of the question, I could either call Liam and most likely have him yell at me, or I could call Lennon. Without thinking about it too much, I hit Lennon's number.

"Hello?" she said after the second ring.

"Hey, Lennon."

"Hey, what's up?" she asked.

"I kind of need a favor from you."

"Is it something fun?" she questioned.

"Well, kind of. I don't want Liam to find out."

"I'll do it!" she immediately shouted through the phone.

"Thank you! I am watching a friend's daughter, and we want to go get ice cream. I was wondering if you could give us a ride?"

"I'll be there in fifteen." She hung up on me.

"Wenna, I want to see your room. Do you have unicorns too?" Sky asked, pulling me away from my phone.

"Let's go and see." With her hand sliding into mine, I led her to my room, her stuff under my other arm.

"You don't have any unicorns! You need unicorns, Wenna!" she said the moment we stepped into my room. Setting her things on my bed, I looked around. My room was pretty plain. It could use some pictures or something. "Don't worry, Wenna, we will get you one." Her soft voice was hard with determination as she nodded, looking around my room.

"I only want one, if you help me pick it out. Maybe we will have to go by a toy store after we get ice cream." Her blue eyes widened, and she nodded excitedly. A minute later, the sound of a knock echoed into my room. Grabbing a pair of flats and my bag, I followed Sky back to the living room. Lennon was already there waiting for us. *Why did she even knock?*

"That was fast," I commented.

"Well, I was already on my way over here. Who

is this beautiful little girl?" she asked, turning her gaze to Sky, who was standing next to me staring at Lennon.

"This is Sky. Sky, this is my friend, Lennon. She is going to come and get ice cream with us."

"Do you like unicorns?" Sky asked, crossing her arms over her chest, a serious look upon her face. Lennon looked at me, but I shrugged at her.

"Of course I do. I like pink ones," she said, squatting down in front of Sky. There was a moment of silence as Sky stared at her, almost as if to make sure she was being serious and to see if she was cool enough to hang with us. She must have found something that she liked, because in a matter of seconds, a wide toothy grin spread across her face.

"Good! Ice cream now!" I shook my head, and Lennon chuckled quietly. We both nodded and headed to the door.

Once we got Sky settled in the back and we were driving down the street, Lennon finally asked me what happened last night.

"Where did you guys go after you left?"

"Nowhere. We just went to McDonald's."

"I thought you were just going to go home?" She glanced over at me for a second before focusing back on the road.

"Well, after I got bombarded with the paparazzi, Liam drove us to McDonald's," I said with a shrug.

"Wait, what? The paparazzi were outside?" Her voice was rising. I glanced over my shoulder to make sure Sky was okay and found her staring out the window.

"Yeah. I walked outside and was swarmed with cameras and people asking me questions about Liam and my engagement. Liam came out a minute later, rescuing me before we jumped in the car and left. I'm surprised you didn't see them when you left the diner."

"How did they find out? And no, they must have left before we got done."

"Garrett told them, apparently," I answered bitterly. It hurt knowing he told when he promised he wouldn't.

"Garrett, as in your driver and the one I met just the other day?"

"Yes. We just got back from McDonald's and we were having a good time until he came and knocked on the door. He and Liam got in a little fight that gave away that I told Garrett about the deal. It was downhill from there. They cornered him yesterday for information and gave him money for it."

"Wow. That is, just wow. I bet Liam was pissed." I sent her a look of warning her that Sky was in the backseat.

"Well he was, and he put me on house arrest. So that is why I called you asking for a ride."

"House arrest, really?" She let out a loud laugh while shaking her head.

"It isn't funny, Lennon. He looked so mad at me."

"Don't worry, Jenna. He will get over it. Just give him a few days. And I am always up for some fun and ice cream." She sent a smile over to Sky and kept driving.

"I hope he does," I muttered softly.

"You know what? We are going to show Sky here a great time!" Lennon said suddenly.

"What do you mean?" I asked.

"You'll see. She's going to love it! You are already in trouble, so you might as well make the most of it," she reasoned. She was right. If I was already in deep shit with Liam, I might as well do this. He was going to hate me either way, and this way I got to go out and have fun with Lennon and Sky. With a smile in my direction, Lennon turned on the radio.

The ride to wherever we were going went by fairly quickly, and we soon pulled into a huge place called Fiesta Fun. Helping Sky out of the car, I stood there, staring at the place wondering where we were exactly.

"This right here is the greatest place to come and have fun," Lennon said dramatically. With Sky's hand inside mine, we followed after Lennon, still slightly confused. The moment we walked in, I took it all in. Off to my right was a big section that had all different kinds of arcade games, and to my left was what looked like a miniature glow-in-the-dark golf course that went all the way to the back. There was a set of doors on the left that led outside, but what was out there I didn't know. There even looked to be other doors on the right, leading to other rooms.

"You can literally do anything you want here. There's miniature golf, both glow in the dark and regular arcade games, laser tag, 3D simulators, and go-karts. There is also a bouncing room for kids." Wow, this place was huge! "Sky, would you like to play miniature golf?" she asked, looking down at her.

"Yes!" came a loud yell, and she started bouncing. Grinning, we made our way to the counter to pay. The next five minutes were spent paying for a pass that let us do three things plus tokens for the arcade, and picking out golf clubs and balls for golf. After much consideration, Sky finally picked a pink-handled club that fit her height, and a pink ball as well. Lennon ended up with a purple one and a purple ball, while I got blue everything.

I'd never played before, but I wasn't an idiot. As we came up on the first hole, Lennon went first, then Sky, who in turn got a hole in one, making her scream and run around us. Miniature golf turned out to be a lot of fun as we moved from hole to hole, each one getting harder. It felt great to go out and do something normal like this. Sky was having so much fun, running from each hole hitting her pink ball before we could even reach her. More than once I caught her picking her ball up and putting it in the hole, and she would play it off like she didn't do it.

We finished the glow-in-the-dark course about thirty minutes later and put our clubs back, heading to do something else. Lennon and I trailed behind Sky, letting her choose what other thing she wanted to do. She chose one of the 3D simulations for little girls. We each got strapped inside, and the ride started with us moving in a field of horses. You could definitely tell this wasn't what Lennon or I would pick. Although the ride was for little girls, it was fun and was pretty funny watching Sky as her face lit up every time we "came" close to a horse. She'd reach her little hands out to try and touch it.

Twenty minutes later, we were back to finding another thing to do. I decided to play a few arcade games and win Sky a stuffed animal in one of the machines. It took me a few tries, but I finally was able to get her a pink teddy bear, which she named after me. Lennon and I played air hockey and Sky watched us, holding her bear to her. Once Sky started to get bored and antsy, we finally took her to the bouncy room. The moment we stepped through the door, she shoved her bear at me and ran off. The room had a few other kids jumping around, but not too many. Lennon and I took a seat kind of in the corner on one of the mats, watching Sky.

"She is a cutie," Lennon said, smiling fondly at her as she bounced, giggling loudly.

"Yes, she is. Her mom has raised her well."

"Who is her mom, anyways?"

"Her name is Candy. She used to work with me at one of my jobs. She was only seventeen when she got pregnant, so she left school and started working. Now she is on her way to be a hair stylist; she is actually there now, taking one of her final tests."

"She sounds like a strong woman," she commented.

"Candy is. I think you have to be when you are a single mother." We sat in silence, watching Sky play around and find new friends.

"What do you think Liam is going to do if he finds out you left the house today?" Lennon asked out of the blue.

"Honestly, probably just yell at me like always,

or insult me. It won't be anything new," I said, shrugging. It wouldn't be. Ever since I had come to know Liam, all he did was be rude to me and not care about my feelings. I didn't expect him to change.

"Jenna, he really is a good guy. It doesn't seem like it now, but he is. Everyone has their baggage."

"Can't he just be nice to me? His baggage can't be that bad," I whined.

"I would tell you, but it isn't my story. One day he will tell you." *When I am out of his life.* She was right, of course, but I couldn't help but want to figure his out. Yes, he didn't know mine, but still…okay, that wasn't a good argument. I sighed, leaning back against the wall. My life had turned into such a mess.

"When do you think she will be ready to go?" I looked up, seeing Sky with a little boy around the same age jumping around and holding hands. *Awww, young love.*

"I give it an hour." I turned to Lennon with a grin. "Thank you, by the way, for doing this. I know it was so sudden, and it means a lot to me."

"No problem. I'm having fun; I like Sky. Plus, this is a lot more fun than what Liam wanted me to do with you today," she commented.

"The manner lessons," I grumbled. "I don't see why he wants me to get help. I can act perfectly fine."

"It's not that he doesn't think you know how to act. It is just the people at those events. They love to pick on anything they can find, and when they find something, they don't let up until you are practically a sobbing mess in front of everyone. He just doesn't want that to happen to you," Lennon reasoned. She sounded exactly like Liam had the other day.

"I guess you're right." I guess I'd better start listening to and trusting Liam more. I was lost in my own thoughts until Lennon said something.

"We've been here two, almost three, hours. We may want to go get ice cream before we head back." I nodded, standing up and calling Sky over. She looked over at us and looked sadly back at her new friend. I watched, smiling as they hugged, and she ran over to us.

"You ready to go and get ice cream?" I asked.

"Yes!" Grinning, I grabbed her Jenna bear and her hand before leaving the bouncy room with Lennon beside us.

While Lennon drove us to an ice cream shop, Sky sat in the back gabbing about her new friend, Nathan. She went on about what they did and random things about him. It was actually really cute, listening to her getting all excited. About ten minutes later, we pulled into a cute place that had an ice cream cone on the side of it. After making sure Jenna bear was okay in the car, all three of us headed inside. Sky bounced on her heels as we waited in line, trying to see what flavors they had over the counter.

Lennon ordered first, getting a strawberry cone. She stepped to the side for us. Seeing as Sky needed help, I lifted her up and onto my hip so she could see the flavors. And, of course, like every little kid, she wanted to try every flavor, making the poor girl behind the counter go everywhere.

"I am so sorry about this," I said after the fifth sampling.

"Don't worry, it happens a lot." The girl smiled at me. "Your daughter is super cute." I froze at that. I had never even thought about having kids, and it was kind of a given that I wasn't going to. I didn't want to do to them what my mother had done to me. I always figured whatever made my mother leave me would pass onto me, and I did not want that to happen to anyone else.

"I want chocolate!" Sky finally said, jerking me back to reality. I rolled my eyes, and the girl scooped a small cone of chocolate ice cream for Sky before handing it to her.

"I'll have mint chocolate chip." We paid and took a seat in a booth so Lennon could eat her cone before driving us home. Only a few licks in, Sky got chocolate all over her face, grinning widely as she licked her cone. She looked like she was in seventh heaven. Knowing it was no use wiping it off just yet, I dug into my ice cream.

Once all three of us were done, I quickly wetted a napkin and wiped Sky's face before we piled back into the car. Surprisingly, the ride back was quiet, and midway home I turned around to make sure Sky was okay. I found her dead asleep. Chuckling quietly, I turned around and shared a grin with Lennon. It was now three in the afternoon, and we had successfully worn her out. We got back to the house a few minutes later, and I slid out quietly.

"Do you need help with her?" Lennon asked, coming around the car.

"It's okay. I got her. You can go home. Thank you so much for today," I said softly, unbuckling the seatbelt and sliding Sky out of the car and into my arms. Clenched in her arms was her bear, and I smiled fondly down at her.

"No problem, I had a blast. Have a good night. I'll probably be over tomorrow." Giving my arm a pat because she couldn't hug me, Lennon sent me one last grin before going back around to the driver's seat.

While Lennon drove off, I awkwardly put in the code for the door and pushed it open with one hand and my butt. Sky snored softly on my shoulder as I quietly shut the door behind me, heading to my room. I was halfway to my room when a loud voice stopped me in my tracks.

"Where have you been?"

Chapter Seventeen

"Where have you been?" I froze, holding a sleeping Sky in my arms. I hadn't expected Liam to be home so soon. Slowly, I turned around and found Liam standing there, his arms folded across his chest. I looked him up and down, finding him really attractive at the moment even though he was staring at me angrily. He was dressed in a dark blue suit jacket and dress pants, a light blue, almost white, dress shirt with a skinny tie around his neck but loosened. His brown hair was slicked back and to the side.

"Jenna, where were you? And who is that?" he asked again and looked down at Sky in my arms.

"I was kidnapping a child," I said sarcastically before I could stop myself.

"Jenna," he warned, his voice hard.

"Liam, chill. I was with Lennon. Let me put her down, then we can talk," I quietly hissed at him. Ignoring Liam, I turned and headed to my room. With one hand, I peeled back my sheets and gently laid Sky down, grabbing her new teddy bear and her

216

other unicorn stuffed animal. I put them around her before pulling the sheets around her little body. I smiled softly down at her and laid a kiss to her forehead before turning around. Silencing a scream that wanted to come out of my mouth, I glared at Liam, who was right behind me.

"What are you doing, sneaking up on me like that?" I hissed at him.

"Who is she?" he asked, ignoring my question completely.

"Her name is Sky."

"Who does she belong to?"

"Jeez, Liam, she isn't a dog." I rolled my eyes. I watched him looking at Sky almost kindly and with curiosity. I decided to mess with him a little bit. "She is mine." Just as I wanted, his head whipped in my direction.

"She is your child!" he all but yelled.

"Quiet down!" I grabbed his arm and hauled him out of the room and closed the door quietly behind me.

"You have a child? When? How?" he sputtered. I bit back a grin as I made my way to the kitchen for a drink. *It's time for a little fun with him.* "I had her during high school," I said, grabbing a glass and getting some water from the fridge.

"So you didn't finish high school? And that is why you had to have those awful jobs," Liam said in realization. I rolled my eyes with my back turned to him. "Wait, so where has she been since you have been here?" I froze but quickly stopped myself.

"She was with a friend."

"Man, I really did choose the wrong girl. You have a fucking daughter!" Turning around, I saw him running his hands through his hair and his mouth wide open. He actually believed that Sky was my daughter. I knew I shouldn't be so happy to see him like this, but I was. "I hope you know she can't stay with us. I don't want a little whiny child running around."

"Hey! Sky isn't whiny. She is very well behaved. It's not like you're home anyways," I shot back.

"Jenna, why did you never tell me you had a daughter?" he said angrily. Okay, never mind, this wasn't going to plan. He was getting really upset about it.

"Good God, Liam, it was a joke!" I finally said.

"What?" He snapped his eyes up at me, confused.

"Sky isn't mine! She is my friend's daughter, and I'm just watching her today," I admitted, staring straight at him.

"She isn't your daughter," he said slowly, like he wasn't getting it.

"Liam, she is four. I would have had to be fourteen! I had barely gotten my period by then." I hadn't really meant for the last part to come out, but oh well. It would just make him even more uncomfortable. If you ever want to make a guy really uncomfortable and stammer around you, then just bring up how you bleed every month.

"I—I—"

"You are not the smartest, are you?" I said, sending him a grin. When he glared at me, I lost my grin and sobered up. "Okay, I'm sorry, Liam, for lying that she was mine. I just wanted to mess with you. I didn't think you would freak out as much as you did."

"It's okay. That was a good one," he admitted, a small smile gracing his lips.

"You know, I thought you got a background check on me before you offered me the deal," I said.

"I kind of did, but not a thorough one." He scratched the back of his neck. "I only knew where you lived, your name, and your jobs. Didn't really think to check anything else."

"You wouldn't be a good CIA person then. But seriously, who wouldn't do a proper background check on someone who they wanted to be their fake wife? I could be a serial killer for all you know."

"I was desperate. I didn't think it through. And you couldn't be a serial killer. You're too little." He moved around me to the fridge and pulled out a beer.

"'I'm too little'? That could be my trick, making people underestimate me, and then I go in for the kill." I raised an eyebrow at him. "Isn't it too early for a beer? And it is a Tuesday."

"Whatever. Well, I need one with what you just pulled on me," he said, rolling his blue eyes at me.

"Yeah, I got you good." I grinned like the Cheshire cat.

"Whatever," he muttered under his breath.

"What are you doing home so early?" I asked, remembering why he was here.

"You wouldn't answer my calls or texts, so I came over." He said it like it was no big deal, but my grin widened at the sound of that.

"Liam Stanford was worried about me." I reached over and poked his arm.

"What? I was not worried about you." He scoffed at me, taking a pull of his beer.

"Yes you were, don't lie!" I prodded him, still grinning. It felt great teasing Liam and getting a reaction out of him. This probably wouldn't happen again, so I was going to take a full advantage.

"Are you hungry?" he asked, changing the subject quickly. I reluctantly let my teasing go. I opened my mouth to answer when my stomach decided to answer for me. That morning I had forgotten to eat before leaving with Sky and Lennon. "That's a yes." Liam shook his head, then started moving around the kitchen. It seemed that after I messed with him about Sky he had relaxed and even become friendly. Of course with him seeming bipolar, that could probably change at the top of a hat.

"What do you want to eat?" he asked, peering into the fridge and looking at me over his shoulder.

"I don't care really," I answered, shrugging.

"How about we just order something?" he offered, closing the fridge and coming to a stop beside me. Ordering something actually sounded really good because I was not in the mood to make anything.

"That sounds good to me. Let's get pizza since we didn't get a chance to have any last night." With a nod, Liam grabbed his phone and tapped away on it. I leaned against the counter, staring at him.

Our relationship was definitely a weird one. One second we were yelling at each other, well, him yelling at me, and the next we were talking to one another like civilized human beings. Everything that happened yesterday seemed to be forgotten or at least put on the back burner. I didn't know if it was because Liam was just in a good mood or my teasing lightened the mood, or if it was because of Sky; I honestly couldn't tell. If I knew how to keep Liam happy or at least not yelling and getting angry, I'd gladly sell my soul for that information. The thought of a year with his attitude and emotions changing at the drop of a hat was already getting old and on my nerves.

"What kind do you want?" he asked, holding his phone to his ear.

"Pepperoni. Sky likes that kind too," I added. He nodded and spoke into the speaker. I stared at him, leaning against the counter. His work clothes hugged his well-defined body. His brown hair was messy from running his fingers through it a second ago. His jaw and cheeks were starting to get a five o'clock shadow, showing that he hadn't shaven in a few days. To me it made him more rugged and handsome, even though that was practically impossible. I bet Liam could make anything look great, even if his hair was bright pink and hanging down to his shoulders while wearing a Speedo.

The longer I stared at Liam, the more I realized he wasn't the worst person to fake marry. I could be stuck with some old, fat guy. Here I had a smart, sophisticated, rich, sexy guy who wanted me to be his fake wife for a year. Someone like him could get any girl he wanted, but instead he chose me, the girl who had no parents, hadn't ever even kissed a guy, and was just a plain-looking girl. In all honesty, Liam could do a lot better, but not me. He was the one who was stuck with my baggage-filled life. Here I was, complaining about having to marry him when in reality he would probably be the only person that would want me, although none of this was real.

"Okay, pizza will be here in about twenty minutes." His deep voice snapped me out of my staring. Blushing, I looked away, hoping he didn't notice I was staring at him the whole time.

"S-sounds good," I stammered out, willing the red in my cheeks to die down.

"Oh, before I forget, tomorrow afternoon we are getting our engagement photos taken." I nodded and stood there awkwardly, glancing around the kitchen. Thankfully the awkward silence was broken when a little voice spoke.

"Wenna, who is that man?" Whipping around, I found Sky standing in the doorway of the kitchen holding both of her stuffed animals in her arms. Her blonde hair was falling out of her pigtails, and her dress was squawky on her body.

"Oh, Sky, this is…" I trailed off, thinking of a term to call Liam.

"I'm her fiancé," Liam butted in.

"What is a bey-once?" Sky asked slowly, saying it wrong. I couldn't help but grin.

"Well, a fiancé is like a boyfriend," I said, walking over to her. "His name is Liam." Looking over my shoulder, I motioned for him to come over.

"Is he nice?" I wanted to say no, but I stopped myself.

"Yes, he is."

"What is your name?" Liam asked, squatting down in front of her and smiling.

"I'm Sky!" she said, grinning brightly at Liam.

"Wow, what a pretty name for a pretty girl." Seeing him smiling and looking at Sky all cutely made my heart swell. Before it sounded like he didn't like children, but seeing this I knew he had a soft spot for them. "What do you have there?" he asked, pointing to her bear and unicorn.

"This Wenna. I just got her today," she said, holding out the brown bear to Liam. "This is Pinky. She's a unicorn."

"They are both very cute."

"You can hold them if you want," Sky said, holding out both and waiting for Liam to take them. Shooting me a look, he took them and held them in his big hands. I grinned, finding the situation very cute.

"Is Wenna named after Jenna?" Liam asked Sky.

"Yes! Wenna is the bestest person ever! Her and Lemon took me to play golf and this jumpy place where I met Nathan and then we got ice cream!" I let out a chuckle at Sky calling Lennon "Lemon."

"Wow, sounds like a great day!" Sky nodded, making more of her blonde hair fall into her face. Just then, the doorbell rang.

"Food is here. Here, Sky, do you want to hold these for me for a second?" he asked, almost giving her puppy dog eyes. She grabbed them and stared at Liam as he went to the door to pay. The way she was staring at him was like he was her knight in shining armor. Looked like Liam had an admirer.

Shaking my head, I grabbed three plastic plates I found in one of the cabinets just as Liam came back with two pizza boxes.

"Pizza!" Sky yelled, running over to the counter where Liam set the boxes. Liam grinned down at her and opened them up.

"Sky, how about we eat these while watching TV? Does that sound fun?" he asked her. She didn't even reply. All she did was nod enthusiastically. Candy was never going to let me watch her again, as I'd spoiled her all day with fun, ice cream, and now pizza while watching TV. Putting a small piece of pepperoni pizza on a plate for Sky, I put one on mine along with the meat lovers from the other one Liam got.

"I got drinks," Liam said.

"Just water or apple juice for Sky. I don't think she needs any more sugar," I said, grabbing our plates along with Liam's and heading to the living room, following Sky. Sky made sure her animals were all comfy on a chair to the side of the couch before she jumped up in the middle of the couch, her legs swinging back and forth.

"Sky, let me know if you can't finish this okay, and if you want more," I said, putting her plate in her lap along with a spread-out napkin; I didn't want anything to get on Liam's expensive couch.

"Here is your drink, my princess," Liam said dramatically, walking into the room and setting a small plastic up on the coffee table with what looked like apple juice. I stared at him, completely baffled at his mood. He was acting the complete opposite of anything I had seen from him prior. He was being sweet, funny, and amazing with Sky. Sky's giggles made me look away, but I kept glancing at him. "And here is yours, Jenna." He handed me a glass with apple juice as well.

"We are all having juice tonight," he said, catching the look on my face. Nodding, I sent him a smile and took a seat with Sky on one side and Liam on the other. He flipped on the TV and started browsing the stations as we munched on our food.

Thankfully, it was our luck a Disney movie had just started. I doubted Liam even had any. It turned out to be *Tangled*, causing Sky to scream. Leaning to my side, Liam and I shared a look before looking at the screen. Throughout the movie, Sky would burst out with random singing, and when Rapunzel started singing "I Have a Dream," she got up, setting her pizza down, and started dancing. Liam and I laughed together, cheering her on as she moved around the living room.

About an hour later, the movie was coming to an end and our pizza was gone. Sky was starting to settle down. It was now almost seven, and I couldn't help but yawn every so often from my lack of sleep from the night before. When the movie finally ended, I sat up, turning to Sky.

"I think it is someone's bath time. Let's go get you bathed and in your PJs," I said.

"I don't want to!" Sky whined, falling back into the couch.

"But princesses aren't stinky," Liam said, looking at her. "If you want to be a princess, you have to bathe and get all clean." Even young girls Liam had a way with. Just one look or word from him, and Sky was hanging onto and staring at him like he was her prince. Sky definitely loved him. Without another word, she jumped off the couch and ran toward my room.

"I have no idea how you do it," I said, shaking my head, staring after her.

"Girls just love me." Liam smirked at me, but it faded into a real grin. I loved seeing his grin. It showed his white teeth, and his blue eyes crinkled a little. "I'll clean this up, and you go get her cleaned." He gestured for me to go while standing up. "By the way, when is her mom coming to get her?"

"Around nine," I answered before heading to my room to bathe Sky.

Almost thirty minutes later, I came out with Sky clad in her blue Elsa PJ dress, and me with my wet jeans and shirt. It took longer to bathe her than I thought. The moment she got in the warm tub, she wouldn't get out. She ended up splashing around and pretending she was a princess saving a fish in the sea. Almost dragging her out of the water after her hands got pruned, I dried her off and slipped on her dress before braiding her blonde hair. While I was in there, Liam cleaned up the pizza and drinks. When I walked in the living room after Sky, I saw he had taken off his shoes and rolled up his dress shirt sleeves, as well as taken off his tie with a few buttons unbuttoned at the top of his shirt. I hadn't even realized both of us were still in our clothes when I sat back down with Sky.

"*Frozen* is about to come on," Liam said the moment my butt hit the couch. With a "yay" from

226

Sky, she had me grab both of her animals before she snuggled against Liam. We watched the entire movie with Sky in Liam's lap with one of her animals in her arms and the other in Liam's. With both of them so engrossed in the movie, I grabbed my phone and made sure the flash was off before snapping a few photos of them without them noticing. Liam seemed to be more into the movie than Sky was, and about twenty-five minutes before the end, Sky passed out in his arms. Once the credits were rolling, Liam looked at me, then at Sky. His face softened as he stared at her, and a smile graced his lips.

"Here, do you need me to take her?" I asked, moving over a little closer.

"It's okay. I got her," he whispered, making sure not to wake her up. I leaned over and smiled, seeing her dead asleep on Liam with her bear clenched in her arms. Looking up, I came face to face with Liam. I hadn't realized how close I had gotten, and we were now inches away from each other. His warm breath blew across my face as his blue eyes stared into my green ones. My lips parted as I stared at him, unknown feelings rushing through me. The way Liam was staring at me made me feel all tingly. My heart was starting to pound in my chest so hard that I was certain he could hear it. I watched as his blue eyes darkened when he glanced down at my lips. My tongue involuntarily ran across my bottom lip as he gazed at them, and his eyes darkened even more.

I had never been this close to a guy before, and with unknown feelings running through my body, I didn't know what to do. The overwhelming need to kiss Liam was starting to consume me. I wanted to know if those light pink lips felt as soft as they looked. I knew I was very inexperienced in that area, but being in such a close proximity to him, all that flew out of my mind and my body moved closer to him. Sky was completely forgotten between us. I didn't know where the sudden urge to kiss him came from, whether it was the way he was acting all night with Sky or what, but I wanted him. No, I needed to kiss him.

Just as I was leaning in and my eyes were starting to close on their own, the sound of the doorbell ringing made us jump apart like we were on fire. Something washed over Liam's face, and he cleared his throat, moving away from me. Breathing hard, the realization of what I was about to do washed over me. I was about to kiss Liam when only the day before I couldn't stand to be around him. I mean, it wasn't like we weren't going to kiss throughout the year since we would have to, but the suddenness of it was what surprised me.

The look on Liam's face as he stared back at me made my heart ache. The mistake that was about to be made was clear on his face, as was his shock. I didn't know what was going on inside of his mind, but the way he was leaning away from me with Sky in his arms was enough for me to tell he wanted to get the hell away from me. *I really must be that unlikeable. That just the idea of kissing me is disgusting.*

The sound of the doorbell ringing again made me jump up and head to the door with weak legs. I heard Liam get up behind me, but I tried to ignore it. Opening the door, I saw Candy standing there, looking tired.

"Hey," she said and went to say something but stopped. I followed her eyes behind me, seeing Liam standing there with a sleeping Sky.

"Candy, this is Liam. Liam, this is Candy, Sky's mother and my friend," I introduced them, but my voice sounded shaky and weird. She opened her mouth to say something, but maybe it was the look on my face that made her close her mouth and hold her hand out to Liam. "Let me go grab her clothes really quick," I said, moving past Liam and running to my room. Making sure I had everything of Sky's, I ran back out and saw Liam and Candy quietly talking.

"Here you go," I whispered, walking up to them, interrupting whatever they were saying.

"Oh thank you, Jenna, for watching her. It means a lot." She took the stuff from my hands and shot me a grateful smile.

"No worries. She is always a blast to hang out with."

"Let me take her to your car," Liam said, and Candy nodded, leading him to her car. He gently laid Sky in the backseat and buckled her up before laying a soft kiss on her forehead. The sight warmed my heart, but I was still shaken up about our almost kiss.

"Thank you," Candy said. "I better get home." Coming over, she gave me a hug and whispered in my ear, "We are definitely talking tomorrow about the hunk. Thank you again for watching her." She pulled away from me.

"No problem. Let me know when you get home." With another thank you to Liam, she got in her car. I stood there, watching her leave, before turning and heading inside. I expected Liam to be inside waiting for me but instead found an empty room. The TV was off and everything. Confused and slightly hurt, I made my way to my room, wondering why Liam ran off so quickly. Seeing his light on down the hall, I froze, pondering if I should go over there. Letting out a sigh, I shook my head and went into my room.

After getting undressed and sliding into bed, I thought about everything that happened tonight. It seemed whatever happened between Liam and me, we would go five steps forward but ten steps back. I lifted a hand to my lips and almost swore they were tingling, although we didn't actually kiss. Everything about Liam confused me but made me want more. Even now I still wanted to know what his lips felt like against mine or trailing down my neck. Shaking those thoughts and everything else about him out of my mind, I closed my eyes, willing myself to sleep, not wanting to think about Liam at all.

Acknowledgements

I want to thank my parents for helping me with this process and for encouraging me to continue writing. Big thanks to my mom for always helping me with names, titles, and for forcing me to sit down and write. I want to thank everyone on Wattpad who has read this story and encouraged me to get it published. It is because of you guys that this book is where it is at today and the reason I still write. You guys are always encouraging me to write and to follow my dreams of being an author. Without Wattpad and everyone on it, I would definitely not be where I am today. And lastly, thank you to my family and friends who are going to go out and buy this book to support me. Knowing that you guys support me in writing and everything else I do in life makes me love you all more than ever. I love you guys so much, and thank you for all you do for me!

About the Author

Currently lives in a small town called Mesquite, Nevada. She is going to college to be an English teacher and writes on the side. When she isn't busy with school work or writing new books she likes to hang out with her family, do things outdoors, and read whatever she can get her hands on.

Facebook:
https://www.facebook.com/kenadee.bryant

Twitter:
https://twitter.com/kendoll350

Goodreads:
https://www.wattpad.com/user/OutOfMyLimit17

42260447R00146

Made in the USA
Lexington, KY
14 June 2019